Books by K. J. Larsen

The Cat DeLuca Mysteries
Liar, Liar
Sticks and Stones
Some Like it Hot
Bye, Bye Love
There Was a Crooked Man

There Was a Crooked M

There Was a Crooked Man

A Cat DeLuca Mystery

K. J. Larsen

Poisoned Pen Press

Library of Congress Catalog Card Number: 2015957976

ISBN: 9781464205897   Hardcover
        9781464204289   Trade Paperback

Poisoned Pen Press
6962 E. First Ave., Ste. 103
Scottsdale, AZ 85251
www.poisonedpenpress.com
info@poisonedpenpress.com

Printed in the United States of America

This one is for sisters everywhere.

Acknowledgments

Our heartfelt thanks to all who helped make *There Was a Crooked Man* possible. To the best papa ever, Harold Larsen. To our sweet mama, Arlene Larsen. If we didn't know you were laughing on the other side, we couldn't write comedy. To our number one sissy, Lynn Lee Higbee. And our dear friends, Alan Mitchell and Amanda Boblet.

A big shout out for the amazing cast at Poisoned Pen Press. And mostly for our extraordinary, long-suffering editor, Barbara Peters. She's no less than magical.

Chapter One

A fierce wind blew off the lake, rattling the catwalk beneath my feet. I hovered fifty feet in the air on a sketchy billboard marked for demolition by the city of Chicago. Shimmying up this godforsaken structure hadn't been one of my smarter moves. But then, being a hotshot detective doesn't mean you have good sense.

I was armed with spy-eyes, a long-focus lens camera, and a Snickers bar. From my vantage point, I had a bird's-eye view of trendy shops and old-time bars in this South Chicago neighborhood. Bridgeport has a funky, friendly vibe and a history rife with gangsters and shady politicians. There's a strong sense of community here and you know your neighbor has your back. If he thinks you want to kill yourself, he's right there cheering you on.

My gaze swept the street below and froze on Johnnie's Grill and Sports Bar. The proprietor, Johnnie Rizzo, is a study in brute testosterone and charm. He's got ravishing brown eyes that suck women in. I was close enough to pitch a rock through his window.

I fell crazy in love with Johnnie the summer I worked at his restaurant. It happened in the walk-in cooler, pressed up against the wall, wedged between a slab of beef and five-gallon buckets of condiments. Johnnie had slow hands and fast fingers. We were married before my feet hit the ground.

A few months into marital bliss I planned a surprise for Johnnie. I sashayed into the cooler all dolled up in high heels, a faux leopard fur coat, and my birthday suit. And there was Johnnie, thrust between the hanging beef and the five-gallon condiments. And a ditzy blond waitress.

Same wall. Different ketchup. Different cow.

That was the day my feet hit the ground and stayed there.

It wasn't long before I discovered I'd married a serial cheater.

My marriage was a bust but it rocket-started my career. Chasing Johnnie Rizzo's cheating ass gave me mad skills. I earned my PI license and launched the Pants On Fire Detective Agency. I don't investigate for law firms or insurance companies and I won't find your lost Uncle Hal. But if you're in Chicagoland and you suspect your partner is stepping out, give me a call.

My name is Cat DeLuca, PI, and I catch cheaters.

◇◇◇

I turned my back on Johnnie's Grill and Sports Bar and set my sights on the brownstone apartment across the street. The wind off the lake clawed at me and the old, wooden bones beneath me shuddered. I said a couple Hail Marys, aimed my spy-eyes and counted the panes of glass. Four floors up, four windows over. Apartment 4B. That's where the "other woman" receives her mail. And an eighteen hundred-smacker Laura Ashley loveseat.

My client, Dorrie Gillet, discovered the charge on her husband's platinum Visa. It was a stunning truffle microfiber loveseat viewed through my binoculars. She'd hired me to track down the loveseat, but I suspect she was more interested in the buns that warmed it.

Dorrie's husband, Sheldon, shows all the signs of a middle-aged cheater. He traded his Prius for a Camaro. He buys gifts she never sees and his little blue pills disappear like candy. He's definitely not rising to the occasion at home.

Last month Sheldon blew a bundle of their savings on a hair transplant. Dorrie showed me before and after pictures. They were amazing. He might have George Clooney hair now. But his face still screams Elmer Fudd.

"I suspect Shelly is cheating on me," she said bitterly.

Seriously? I glanced at the photo of Elmer again. "Have you talked to him about it?"

"He laughed at me. He said I was imagining things."

That's what they all say.

Her lips pursed in an angry line. "Sheldon is a church deacon, for God's sake. I told our pastor he's catting around. I said, 'Shelly's going to hell.'"

"What did your pastor say?"

"He said Sheldon's experiencing a mid-life crisis. That God wants me to forgive him."

I didn't trust myself to respond. I whipped out my Dr. Pepper Lip Smacker and smeared my mouth.

"When hell freezes over," Dorrie said. "That's what I said to the pastor. I told him God wants Sheldon to keep his pants zipped."

I tucked the Lip Smacker in my jeans' pocket. Her eyes had a hard, terrifying glint. I almost expected her head to start spinning.

"I've been a good wife to that man."

"What do you want from me?"

"I want you to find out where that loveseat was delivered."

"Okay."

"And then torch it."

I smiled. "Sorry. I don't—"

"But you know someone who does." One crazy eye winked. "And I want hard evidence that I can slap in Sheldon's face. One photograph of the lying bastard to prove I'm not bat-shit crazy."

That could take more than a photo. Or maybe not.

I considered her cray-cray eyes thoughtfully. Perhaps she wasn't so bat-shit after all. Dorrie Gillet's life, as she knew it, was unraveling. She felt betrayed. She was pissed off. But mostly she was scared shitless.

In this business, I meet people on their very worst days.

I touched her hand. "I'll find out the truth about your husband. And I'll get your photo. My 8 by 10 glossies will clear or convict him."

She found a tissue in her bag and blew her nose. It sounded a lot like a foghorn.

"I am a just Christian woman."

"I know."

"And I will choke the thankless fornicator in his sleep."

"Uhm…"

Dorrie slapped a wad of cold hard cash on my desk. "We never had this conversation. I was never here."

And just like that, *Poof!* She wasn't.

◇◇◇

I had been stalking the thankless fornicator for days and he'd been on his best behavior. But that ship was about to sail. Today I followed Sheldon after work to his lover's brownstone. Her name is Michelle and she's a sous chef at a French bistro in Hyde Park. She likes retro furniture and peppermint patties. She props an insane number of stuffed toys on her bed. She wears baby-doll lingerie. There was a home pregnancy test in her waste basket. Negative. And the loveseat is amazing.

I know this because I broke into Michelle's apartment when she was at work. I got her address from the delivery guys at Walter E. Smithe. They remembered the loveseat, all right. Maybe because they hoisted it four miserable flights up a narrow, sweat-box stairway without so much as a tip or a thank you. I gladly gave them both.

I was in Michelle's apartment when I decided to climb the billboard for my photo-op. The structure is mildly treacherous but it's a straight camera shot to Michelle's bedroom window. I waited in my car for Sheldon to enter his lover's apartment. Then I crossed my fingers, made my peace with God, and jumped the yellow police tape.

I aimed my long focus lens camera at Apartment 4B across the street. Michelle's menagerie of stuffed animals had been moved to three shelves. Elmer Fudd sprawled on the bed alone, head propped on a pillow, wearing a pair of stars and stripes bikini briefs. It appeared another little blue pill had been activated for takeoff.

Sheldon had the soft, undeveloped body of a guy who was never into sports and spends too many weekends on the couch. He may have been captain of the debate team in school but he would've been the last kid picked for sports. He didn't have a lot of body hair, just a few honey-gold tufts around his man-breasts.

"Come on," I whispered.

As if on command, Michelle emerged from the bathroom in a soft pink baby doll and white fishnet stockings. She had long black hair and skin like caramel. She may not have Sheldon's generous breasts but she's an attractive woman in her own right with firm, wide hips and a round, shapely caboose. She danced for him slowly, gliding around the bed with an easy, sensual motion. Her fingers explored her skin and she danced as if she was making love to her body.

I focused the camera lens.

"Say cheese."

Click.

Her hips sashayed seductively and her arms were fluid as melted butter. She stripped for Elmer, removing her spaghetti straps slowly, one by one, until all she wore was a delicate gold anklet with diamond and ruby hearts.

Click.

Elmer Fudd's eyes bulged. He appeared as if his face would explode.

Click. Click.

His eyebrows darted up and down and beads of sweat dribbled from his George Clooney hair. He watched her dance until he couldn't contain himself a moment longer. Then he pulled her on the bed and kissed her hard before pushing her onto her knees. Michelle's long black hair draped the stars and stripes, and the rocket's red glare. And then Chef Michelle served up one of her French specialties.

I smiled. "Say Brie."

Click. Click. Click.

A hefty gust of wind blew off the lake and the billboard's wooden frame shuddered beneath me.

"It's a wrap," I said.

I took a bite of my Snickers and tucked the camera and binoculars into my shoulder bag. A shrill voice squawked from the street below.

"Jumper! We've got a jumper!"

Jumper? My eyes swept the surrounding rooftops. Nada.

"Jump! Jump!"

I looked down at the street where a small crowd was gathering. My heart sank. They were yelling at me.

OMG!

"Jump! Jump!" An obnoxious guy chanted. A small chorus of doom joined in.

"I'm a city inspector!" I shouted but no one heard. They were having too much fun yelling at me.

"Hold on, Dearie!" an old woman called. The cops are on their way!

Crap!

I began retracing my steps to the ladder, carefully negotiating the catwalk. A crowd of looky-lous poured out of Johnnie's Sports Bar. They heard there was a jumper and they were pumped for a bloodbath.

I moved quickly, making my way to the ladder. An all-too-familiar voice called to me. My feet froze and my stomach lurched.

"Kitten, stop!" Johnnie Rizzo bellowed. "I know you love me! Don't jump! You can get over us!"

"Holy crap!"

"Ha!" I blubbered. I was stunned by the enormity of that man's ego.

Johnnie wailed. "I'm not worth it."

"Captain Obvious has arrived, ladies and gentlemen!" I shot back.

"Come down, Kitten! You don't want to die!"

"I'm not jumping, fool!"

I scanned the crowd. Phones were held high in the air, videotaping. I groaned. My foiled suicide attempt and my Johnnie

Rizzo heartbreak would certainly hit YouTube, if not the evening news.

"All right," my ex cried, "I'm coming up for you."

Johnnie Rizzo is terrified of heights. His offer was enormously brave. And, I reluctantly admitted, rather sweet.

"Go, Johnnie, go!" The bar crowd chanted. They were louder than the *Jump* mob. Johnnie sucks people in. They love him.

"No, Johnnie, no!" I yelled, scampering for the ladder. "I'm coming down!"

Johnnie's two hundred pounds might easily bring this billboard to its knees. I reached the ladder and began descending the steps.

The ladder brought me most of the way down. The final twenty feet I slid down a pole.

The nice people cheered. The *Jump!* crowd booed. And the *Go Johnnie Go* bunch dissolved into the restaurant to freshen their drinks.

Sirens screamed. The cops were on their way.

Before my feet hit the ground, Johnnie caught me in his arms. He was trembling and his eyes were wet.

"Thank God," he breathed. His big brown eyes searched my face and he locked onto my eyes with his. I shuddered. He was sucking me in.

Damn those eyes. I took a breath and pushed him away. "I wasn't going to jump."

"Of course you weren't." He didn't believe me for a moment. "Okay, Kitten. You got what you wanted. You have my attention."

"I wasn't trying to—*arrrgh!*"

I looked down the street. Flashing lights barreled down on us. Sirens screamed.

"Gotta run."

"For God's sake, Cat, get some help. See a shrink or something. If money's a problem, business has been good. I've got what you need."

"You're such an egotistical jackass."

I hightailed it toward my car as the first patrol cars screeched to the curb. My crazy Cousin Frankie jumped out first, hand on holster, always ready to shoot someone.

"Hi, Frankie!" I waved.

"Cat!" His head jerked side to side. "Did you see the jumper? Where did she go?"

I pointed down the street. "She ran into Johnnie's."

Frankie roared into his radio and a mass of blue swarmed Johnnie's Sports Bar and Grill.

I looked over my shoulder at Johnnie. He shook his head and dragged a hand through his hair.

"Not cool, Kitten."

But his big, woman-sucking eyes were smiling.

Chapter Two

I put the billboard in my rearview mirror and drove to Tino's Deli. Tino is one of Bridgeport's most intriguing residents. He's an ex-spy and his current relationship with the government is just one of his many secrets.

Tino met me at the door and threw his big bearlike arms around me. "Ah, Caterina. You didn't hurl yourself off the billboard, after all." He winked. "Unless you can fly."

I didn't ask how he heard. Tino knows stuff. You just accept it. If you think about it too much, it gets creepy.

I made a face. "The crowd was vicious. Some wanted me to jump."

"Give me names. I'll poison their sausage."

"They were the McDonald's crowd."

"They're getting a slow poisoning already."

I laughed.

Tino's eyes danced. "Whose bedroom did you intrude upon up there? Was the woman a beauty?"

"You know I never click and tell."

"Can I see your dirty pictures? Just a little peek?"

"Nice try." I gave his arm a playful slap and searched the display case. "Am I too late for tiramisu? I was hoping to get some for tomorrow night."

"Ah. Savino's coming for dinner." Chance's lust for tiramisu is legendary. "I have some in back. Made fresh this morning."

Tiramisu is a creamy, Italian, mocha-trifle that's heaven in your mouth. It tantalizes your tongue with an explosion of chocolate and liqueur.

Tino brought the dessert from the kitchen and I drooled like Pavlov's dog.

"It looks divine."

"If you want, I have a nice bottle of Sambuca for a nightcap."

"Perfect."

"Sambuca's an aphrodisiac. Savino will be late for work tomorrow."

He opened a white paper bag and placed the tiramisu and the Sambuca inside. He added a handful of sausages.

"For Inga. Your mama came by for some this morning. But in this life, you can't have too much love. Or too many sausages."

I hugged him and my fingers barely touched behind his back. Tino has put away a lot of sausages since his spy days. He's a bigger target than he once was. But he keeps an eye over his shoulder and he drives a bulletproof car.

His dark eyes glinted. "A birdie tells me your first anniversary is next week."

I frowned. I hadn't told anyone.

"Spill it," I said.

"Your mama."

I groaned. "If Mama knows, everyone knows."

"Pretty much. What is this anniversary you celebrate? Not your first date, I think. This is the day you and your FBI agent sealed the deal?"

My cheeks felt hot.

"Ah. *Amore.*"

He opened a bottle of Chianti and breathed deeply. The rich, fruity fragrance filled my nostrils.

"To a long life and good health." He splashed wine in two glasses. "*Due dita di vino e una pedata al medico.*"

It was an old Italian saying, one my Nonna toasted every day. I raised my glass to her.

"A little wine kicks the doctor out the door."

◇◇◇

The year I lost two hundred pounds of runaround Johnnie Rizzo and launched the Pants On Fire Detective Agency, Uncle Joey fixed me up with a brick bungalow. The house is on a large, corner lot with a spray of maples and a patio garden in back. I fell in love with it at once. Uncle Joey negotiated the sale and I got it for a song. When I asked why it came so cheap, he said I didn't want to know. Trust me, when Joey tells you that, you usually don't.

Uncle Joey is, in the long tradition of DeLuca men, a Chi-Town cop. Ever since my great-grandfather, Officer Antonio DeLuca, conspired with Al Capone to bootleg whiskey, the DeLuca men have protected and served the good citizens of Chicago. They raise families in Bridgeport and hang out at a cop bar called Mickey's. Most are honest cops and a few have deep pockets. But Uncle Joey is special. He drives a red Ferrari and wears tailor-made Italian suits. He's got the Midas touch.

I'm not saying my uncle's a dirty cop. I like to think he's resourceful. Uncle Joey has friends in low places. I'm not privy to their hijinks and I don't ask him how he turns copper to gold. It's not my business. And even if it was, I wouldn't say anything. If there's one thing we DeLucas understand, it's how to keep our big mouths shut.

I'll probably never know why my house was a steal. On an eerie night when the wind howls, I wonder if one of Joey's badass friends buried a body in the basement. Or maybe deep in the garden beneath the blood-red roses. That's when I light a candle, burn a little sage, and remind myself that before I moved in, Father Timothy doused the crap out of the place with holy water. Then I rest in peace.

I drove home and when I stepped inside, a beagle charged full bore from the kitchen, leash dangling from her teeth. Inga's my partner at the agency. She's smart with a shrewd nose for crime. Left unchecked, she's likely to eat the evidence.

I knelt and scratched her ears. "Give me fifteen minutes and we'll go for a run. I want to print these pics for our client."

Inga flashed a goofy grin and led the way to my office. I slipped the memory card from my camera into the laptop and rows and rows of Sheldon's soft man breasts appeared on the screen. Yikes. Curly, honey-colored tufts of hair circled the nipples. I chose a half dozen poses from pole girl's gyrating hips to circus girl riding her Sheldon pony. Then I printed the 8 by 10 glossies, and tucked them inside a manila envelope.

Delivering the evidence can be the most difficult part of a hotshot PI's job. My clients hire me to confirm or negate their suspicions. When a suspected partner proves faithful, I buy a bottle of champagne and happy-dance to my client's door. But when the pics expose betrayal, it's devastating for the jilted lover. And gut-wrenching for the messenger, as well.

I tied my hair in a ponytail and changed into soft peach velour sweats and running shoes. Inga darted ahead and waited at the door. I snapped up the Frisbee and yellow envelope. "We'll play in the park before running these pics to our client's house."

Inga made a face.

"I don't expect tears from this client. Dorrie's a no-nonsense woman. We might have to dissuade her from taking an ax to her husband."

Inga's white-tipped tail beat the door. I reached for the knob and heard the metallic clink of a key turning the lock. The tail wagged harder.

"You're fired as a watchdog."

The door opened and Mama swept inside bearing gifts. Inga howled joyfully and Mama squeezed her cheek.

"Sausage for my favorite grand-dog."

She stuffed a fat one in Inga's mouth. Inga groaned and her eyes rolled back in her head.

Mama dangled the Tupperware in my face. "For you, Caterina, cannoli. Drizzled in chocolate."

My fave. A yummy sound almost escaped my lips. I choked it back down and narrowed my eyes. Mama widened hers, all innocent like.

"What's going on, Mama? You cut me off. You said no cannoli for a month."

"Did I?"

"You were mad as a wet cat. I skipped a meeting you set up with Father Timothy. You told him I want to reserve the church for a wedding."

Mama wagged a finger. "It's not nice to stand up a priest."

"But—"

"I forgive you." Mama thrust the Tupperware in my arms. I should've stuffed it back in hers but I couldn't bring myself to. Yet I resisted cradling the container greedily.

Mama is, hands down, the best cook in South Chicago. Her unrivaled cannoli can drop a grown man to his knees. Food is Mama's power. She uses it to keep her brood close. There are two hundred and thirty-seven square miles of Chicagoland real estate, and Mama sucks her five kids in. We can almost smell her ciabatta baking from our porches.

She is ruthless.

I flashed my left hand in her face. "No diamond. There's no wedding. Savino and I are not engaged."

Mama clutched a hand to her chest. It's her heart attack pose. The doctor says it's gas.

"Don't set appointments for me with Father Timothy." I glanced down at the cannoli and saw I was hugging it. "Please," I added more gently.

I carried the Tupperware into the kitchen and tucked the cannoli in the refrigerator. Mama poked her head in and made a disapproving clicking sound with her mouth. I hadn't gone shopping and my fridge was quite bare. There was lipstick on the grape juice container.

Another perk of the single life.

I wiped the lipstick from the carton and poured Mama a glass. Then I found the Tums and pressed two in her hand.

"Take the Tums, Mama. Your heart will feel better."

"I'll feel better when my daughter has a wedding."

I tried to look sympathetic. It's tricky to pull off when you want to choke someone.

"You're no spring chicken, Caterina DeLuca. You're thirty-one years old. Your eggs, they shrivel and dry up. And then what? Where are my grandchildren?"

"I gave you Inga."

She made a clicking sound with her tongue. "If this FBI agent isn't man enough to ask you, marry Max instead."

"Max isn't Italian. His family eats lutefisk at Christmas."

"No pasta?" Mama's hand fluttered to her heart. "What is this lutefisk?"

"It's fish. Cod, actually. Soaked in lye."

Mama gasped. "That man will not poison my grandchildren."

I laughed. "Take the Tums, Mama."

"I talked to Mrs. Savino."

"Chance's mama?" I gulped. "God, no."

"Mrs. Savino tells me you don't want to marry her son."

"Boundaries, Mama. For heaven's sake."

"I told Mrs. Savino about your shriveling eggs."

"Oh, God."

"She should talk to her son. I said you might marry the dentist I told you about. He asked about you again the other day. You'll save a fortune on your children's teeth."

My head began to ache. The truth is, Savino has brought up marriage several times. But I've managed to dodge the subject. Marriage didn't work well for me the first time around. And I like things as they are. I'm perfectly happy with my own eccentric, interfering family. The thought of adding Chance's parents to the mix makes me nauseous.

"Tick tock," Mama added under her breath, all hushed and subtle-like, hoping I'd think I was hearing my biological clock.

I massaged my temples. "I know that was you, Mama."

"Johnnie Rizzo was no good for you. He hurt you bad. It's time to give another man a chance."

"I've moved on," I said but my voice lacked conviction.

I had been shell-shocked when I learned my husband was an incurable cheater. I hired a lawyer, moved home with my parents for a few months, got my PI license, and launched the Pants On Fire Detective Agency. The day I was to sign a lease on an apartment, Uncle Joey said he had a house to show me. When I walked through the door, I knew I was home.

I love my life. I've built a successful career, but the nature of the work can be emotionally brutal. I stalk cheaters and my perspective on marriage takes a beating every day. Had I really moved on? Maybe I had been too controlled when I dissolved my ties to Johnnie. Perhaps if I'd chased his sorry bum down and filled it with buckshot, like Cleo did to Walter, I'd have exorcized my rage. At least my stomach wouldn't lurch every time Chance brought up the M word.

The Tupperware of cannoli was a bribe. Mama wanted something and she hadn't shown her hand.

"I don't have much time, Mama. I'm meeting with a client in a few minutes. Do you need something?"

"You have to talk to your sister."

I groaned. My sister, Sophia, is a Barbie doll baby factory who sucks up to Father Timothy and still gets me in trouble with our parents. She disrespects me and she hates the Pants On Fire Detective Agency. I'm pretty sure my parents brought the wrong kid home from the hospital.

"Tell me the truth, Mama. Sophie was switched at birth, wasn't she?"

Mama's eyes were troubled. "I worry about Sophie. There's something bad going on. I want you to talk to her."

"Sophie should talk to Father Timothy. She's always sucking up to him."

Mama snorted. "What does a priest know about a woman's needs?"

"Ha! Remember that next time you go blabbing to Father Timothy about me."

Mama clutched her chest. "You take dirty pictures. You break your mama's heart. Priests know about such things."

I stared at her for a moment. "Why don't *you* talk to Sophie?"

"I tried and she started to cry. She won't tell me. It's girl-talk."

"The last time we did girl-talk was in junior high school. I told her I had a crush on Billy Bonham and she wrote it all over the school bathroom. And on my locker in the hallway. The principal hauled me into the office for choking her. Like *I* was the bad one."

"It's her husband." Mama's voice broke. "I think Peter is straying."

I almost laughed. "Peter? No way. He's been head over heels for Sophie since second grade. This is my profession. And I can promise you, there is no way that guy is cheating."

Mama wasn't listening. "Sophie has babies," she wailed. "What will she do if he leaves her?"

I put my arms around her and kissed her cheek. "Don't worry, Mama. I'll talk to her."

"I can always count on you."

"Somewhere out there there's a crazy family who brought my real baby sister home from the hospital. We should find her."

Mama clicked her mouth. "Sophia has my mama's eyes."

"Shhh." I put a finger to my lips. "That's crazy talk."

I grabbed the Frisbee and 8 by 10 glossies and set the security alarm. The three of us walked outside together.

"I'll call Sophie tomorrow," I said.

"Your sister will be here tomorrow at two. I told her you're planning something special."

I opened my mouth and nothing came out.

Mama scooted to her car and Inga tried to follow her. I jerked her leash.

"Did you hear what she said? That was so manipulative."

She cranked up the Buick and backed out of the driveway.

I stomped a foot. "You can't make appointments for me!"

Mama pretended not to hear me. She waved and drove away.

"I'm taking that kiss back," I called after her.

Chapter Three

The early summer days are long and sweet in Chicago. Dorrie Gillet was pruning her roses when Inga and I jogged over with my 8 by 10 glossies. Her gaze locked on the manila envelope in my hand and she began whacking the bush blindly. I was pretty sure I heard the roses screaming.

"Whoa, Lorena Bobbit. Let go of the scissors."

She delivered a final, vicious blow before dropping the pruners and snatching the envelope from my hand. Bypassing the metal clasp, she shredded the envelope flap with trembling fingers. When she dragged the photos into the sunlight, she gave a strangled gasp.

The French chef's head was buried in Elmer Fudd's lap.

I spoke gently. "I'm sorry to say that Sheldon is…"

"—a dead man," she hissed.

I made sympathetic sounds with my tongue.

"That pig!" She waved a photo in my face. "Do you see that?"

I studied Sheldon's ample body, glistening with sweat. He was an oinker, all right.

She followed my gaze and shoved the photo in my face. "I'm talking about *her*! The bitch stole my diamond ankle bracelet."

Seriously? I whipped out the Dr. Pepper Lip Smacker and smeared. I didn't say Shelly was the sticky-fingered re-gifter. Inga pulled back on her leash, eyes wide with alarm. She wanted to make a break for it. I couldn't blame her. The shearers were dangerously close. And the roses appeared terrified.

I kicked them under a lilac bush.

Dorrie's voice broke. "Shelly gave me that diamond-heart anklet for my birthday. He was furious when I told him I'd lost it."

I bit my tongue. Elmer Fudd was a self-serving, calculating douche bag.

Her raging eyes narrowed. "What happened to her, anyway? I know she didn't go to prison. No woman on a jury would convict her."

"Who?"

"Scissor lady. Lorena B."

Dorrie had the crazy eyes going. I steeled my own and held hers.

"Firing squad. Scissor lady was a bloody mess."

"Liar! You don't want me to go off on the cheater!"

"That's true. You've given him enough of your life. He doesn't get any more."

Her voice oozed bitterness. "Shelly took the best years of my life."

"No way. Your best years are ahead of you."

She looked deflated, as if the wind had been sucked out of her. Her eyes were on the ground, probably searching for her shearers. I put my hands on her shoulder and made her look at me. Then I gave her a good shake and released her.

"You're not a victim. It'll be tough at first but you're smart. You'll figure it out."

She gnawed her lip. "Can I call you sometime? I may need some advice."

"Call anytime. I don't have a lot of advice. I can only tell you what worked for me. Make a bucket list. Do everything you've dreamed of. Be gloriously happy. When you're ready to date again, go out there and rock it. Living well is the best revenge."

She was quiet a long time. When she spoke again, her voice was clipped and strong. The old Dorrie was back. She had a plan.

She stuffed the pics back in my hands and dug the pruners out from under the lilacs. Inga and I took a cautious step back, poised to make a run for it.

She gave a conspiratorial wink. "Keep these photos until I'm ready for them."

"Oh-kay."

"I want copies for Reverend Forgive-The-Shit. And for Shelly's fellow deacons. His pissy mother. And for—hell, I'll just make a list. I'll e-mail pics to his staff at work. It's more efficient, don't you think?"

Ouch. I actually felt sorry for Elmer Fudd.

Hell hath no fury…

Dorrie Gillet gave a tender clip to her battered roses. "I need a little time. I have an expensive bucket list. And there are a few bank accounts to empty first."

"You have my number."

◇◇◇

I woke the next morning to vague dreams of Elmer Fudd strung up by the neck over a bed of screaming roses. The dream put me in a funk that a hot shower and double espresso couldn't touch. I grabbed Inga's leash and we ran the dream into the ground.

We walked down South Halsted, breathing gratifying whiffs of dim sum, and churrasco, and chicken and waffles. Bridgeport offers some of Chicago's best cuisine. It's an orgy for the nose. Despite a bucket list that reads like a stack of travel brochures, there's no place I'd rather come home to.

My first stop was a funky shop that sells incense and those salt candles that are supposed to ward off negative spirits. I bought two large candles for my front porch on the off-chance they'd make my sister disappear. Our next stop was the bakery. I wanted to pick up a little something for my sister's visit. I filled a white bag with a few donuts, fruit tarts, and anisette toast. Lemon tarts are Sophie's favorite but she rarely indulges. When it comes to food, even chocolate doesn't sing to her. She may not be fully human.

Sophie might be a twenty-nine-year-old baby factory but she looks like sweet-sixteen Barbie. She nibbles on rabbit food and tortures herself with Billy Blanks' Boot Camp DVDs. She's perpetually pregnant, or nursing, or both. I doubt she remembers the last time a nice red wine filled her glass.

Today was a rare moment in Sophie-world. My sister wasn't pregnant and a baby wasn't attached to her nipple. It was a flippin' miracle and one she should celebrate with a spa day, a date night with her husband, and a pitcher of margaritas with her sister. I'd happily throw in a year's supply of birth control. Even Barbie deserves a stiff drink and worry-free sex.

Sophie and I are polar opposites. We're like night and day. Oil and water. A Kardashian afternoon. When we're together, our time is strained at best. It's not rocket-science to understand why. We share no genes. My alleged sister, Sophia Maria DeLuca, was switched at birth.

Here are the facts.

I'm tall like my brothers and I adore Serena Williams. Sophie's short and disapproves of women sweating in public. I climbed trees when we were kids. Sophie had a gazillion dolls and she cut holes in their lips to force-feed them. She gave them baths. The day I held Rosie under water, Sophie sobbed. In my defense, I was five and thought her dolls had superpowers.

The last thing Sophie and I had in common was diapers.

Inga and I breezed out of the bakery with goodies in hand. Across the street, a woman outside Baumgarten Jewelry caught my eye. Something about her intrigued me. At first I thought it was her green scarf, covering her red hair. A Hermès original and deliciously gorgeous. She wore a butterscotch leather jacket and her diamond earrings blinged in the sun. She appeared fascinated with a window display of teardrop diamond necklaces. But her posture was too attentive for a dreamy necklace gape. She was on high alert, aware of everything around her. In the window's reflection, I caught her eyes sweep the street behind her. That's when I knew what drew me to her. She was me. Or more accurately, PI Cat DeLuca in surveillance mode.

The woman in green was a professional. A private investigator. An undercover Fed. A government spy. Or even a thief.

Cops and robbers have a lot more in common than you may think.

She seemed to intuit my radar on her and stiffened almost imperceptibly. Her eyes found me in the glass. I smiled and knelt beside Inga, fussing with her collar. She resumed her bogus fascination with the necklaces in the window.

And then my eyes hooked a real skulker and I forgot about the woman in green. He was behind the wheel of a parked Lexus. A hand half-covered his face and he hunkered down in his seat as if willing himself invisible. His shoulders sagged. His right tires flanked a fire hydrant.

He was a picture of doom.

I patted Inga's head. "We're going in, girl. Somebody needs a donut."

We hoofed it to the man's car unobserved. I whipped open the passenger door and hopped inside. Inga clambered over my lap and into the backseat. I dropped the gift bag at my feet and the bakery bag on my lap.

"Why so bummed, Bobby boy?"

Captain Bob flinched and blew a sigh. I'd startled him. And he's a tough guy. He's not one to get rattled.

"Christ, Cat."

Bob Maxfield is Captain of Bridgeport's Ninth Precinct. I had few illusions that he'd be happy to see me. Even on a good day, he forgets how much he loves me. And this was clearly not a good day.

A few decades ago, Bob and Papa were partners, cruising the streets of Bridgeport. Their careers took different paths but they've remained close. Bob is family. He's attended every important milestone in my life. And now he's like the codgy old uncle who hates what I do. Bob is a cop snob. He disrespects private investigators and he calls me a hootchie stalker.

And yet, I bring him donuts. I need therapy.

I glanced at Bob's laptop, open on his lap. A blond Pomeranian cowered on the screen, captive in an unforgiving metal cage. His big brown eyes were pleading. He could've been on death row. A cardboard sign propped beside the cage had something scrawled in black marker. September 19, 1999. I thought it was a photo until the little guy blinked. He was on live feed.

Bob slammed the laptop shut.

I caught my breath. "That was Sam I Am."

"You didn't see that."

"Your dog is in that horrible cage. What's going on?"

"None of your business. Get out of my car."

"My God, Captain. Did some monster kidnap your dog?" Inga whimpered in the backseat.

"Go away, Cat. I got this."

"You don't got shit, Bob. Cuz you don't have Sam."

"I can't hear you."

"Who knows about this?"

"Peggy's in Connecticut. Her sister had surgery."

"You're not alone anymore. You have me now."

He choked a little.

"I'm a trained investigator, Bob. I'll get Sammy back."

"You're a hootchie stalker."

"That hurt, Bob, but I'll let it slide. You're in shock." I opened the white bag and held it for him. "Have a donut."

He scooped up the entire bag, peered inside and frowned. "No lemon crèmes?"

"Lemon tarts."

"That works."

He dragged out a tart and a bear claw and placed them both on the dash.

"Coffee?"

"At my house."

I reached over the console to grab a donut for myself. Bob closed the bag and stuffed it between him and the door.

"You should've brought coffee."

"How much do they want for Sam I Am?"

"They haven't made any demands yet."

"If it's not money they want, why did they take him?"

"Again, none of your business."

The glob of lemon curd on Bob's nose was disturbing. I tried not to stare.

"September 19th, 1999. What does that mean?"

Bob's face twitched and the lemon jiggled. "I don't know."

"Do not try to play poker."

The lemon tart was history. He chomped into the bear claw.

"I bet Papa remembers. You two were partners then."

"Do not involve Tony."

"Why do I have a feeling he's already involved?"

Suddenly Bob looked old and tired. "God, you're irritating. Go away before I have you arrested."

"You have to trust somebody. If you don't want to talk to me, talk to my brother, Rocco. He's a DeLuca. He'll take your secret to the grave with him."

Bob shook his head and his jowls wobbled. "I won't involve my men. If this goes south, I'm not taking Rocco down with me."

"You're making a big mistake, Bob. Huge."

My eyes wandered across the street. The woman in green had moved inside the jewelry store. The proprietor whipped out a black velvet cloth and laid out a tempting selection of diamond necklaces on the counter. I whipped out my pocket spy-eyes.

Bob blew an exaggerated sigh. "My God, Caterina. You're incurable."

"I'm a professional, Captain. We're in the same business."

He gave a hoot. "When pigs fly."

The woman carefully selected a necklace from the counter and handed it to the jeweler. She unbuttoned her leather jacket exposing a long neck and plunging neckline. Push-up bra on steroids. The jeweler ogled appreciatively and stepped behind her. She whipped up her long red hair, holding it on top of her head as he fastened the necklace. As she lowered her hands, a deft finger snared a necklace from the counter. In one fell swoop, it dropped neatly into her pocket.

She fingered her hair and flashed a flirtatious smile at the jeweler. He grinned like an adolescent boy and produced a mirror. They studied the diamonds and sapphires blinging on her breasts. She sighed deeply and gave a regretful shake of her head. Woman in Green wasn't buying the necklace.

"Oh my God, Bob. Did you see that? That woman just stole a diamond necklace."

"I doubt that very much."

"It's in her pocket. I saw her take it with my eyes. Captain! Arrest her."

"You arrest her. Leave me alone."

"You'd like that, wouldn't you?"

There was a rap on the window and one of Bridgeport's finest bellowed through the glass.

"Move it, buddy. You're illegally parked beside a fireplug."

Captain Bob lowered the window and the officer gulped. "Uh, sorry, Captain. I didn't recognize you, sir."

Tommy is a rookie from Wisconsin. He and I became fast friends his first day on the job, when a little explosion in my car almost killed him.

Tommy's gaze drifted to me. Back to Bob's growly face. And to me again. His eyes blinked.

"Sir, is there something I can help you with?"

"Yes, Officer," Captain Bob barked. "Go around to Ms. DeLuca's door and remove her from my car. With force, if necessary."

"Force, sir?"

"You have a gun, don't you? I'll give you a donut if you shoot her."

"Sir?"

Inga and I didn't take our chances. We tumbled onto the sidewalk without assistance.

I poked my head back in the car. "We'll talk tonight, Captain."

"No, we won't."

I lowered my voice to a whisper. "And don't worry about your boy. I'll get him back before Sam I Am becomes Sam I Was."

Chapter Four

Inga and I ran the rest of the way home. I drank a glass of water and freshened the water in her dish. She ate a sausage and I finished off yesterday's Snickers. I took a quick shower with olive oil soap and lavender shampoo and wrapped my hair in a towel.

Then I called Rocco.

Rocco is my brother and he's been my best friend since I can remember. He's married to Maria, a very cool woman, and they have two daughters I adore. I go to all their games and concerts and we have sleepovers and do Disney World. My doting relationship with them seems to satisfy any mother-genes I may have. At least for now.

Rocco picked up on the first ring.

"Yo, Cat. Maria's been bugging me to call you."

"Why doesn't she call me?"

"She doesn't want to get mixed up in, and I quote, 'your insane family's shit.'"

"I'm jealous she has the option. What's Mama plotting now?"

"This can't come back to me."

"Gee, Rocco. You're a great big man and Mama still scares you."

"Mama scares everybody."

"You got that right. Spit it out."

"Our Mama and Savino's mama are planning a surprise party for your anniversary next week."

"What?"

"Your anniversary. You know, it's been a year since you and Chance have been doing the…"

"Oh. Hell, no!"

"Anyway, the Savinos are invading Chicago. There's family coming in from Massachusetts and New York. And a retired aunt from Arizona or something."

"Shut up."

"The family chartered a boat and a crew. It's gotta be a big one for their family and ours. You didn't tell me the family has a helluva lot of money."

"I don't care if…" A pause. "How much money are we talking about?"

"Bouco bucks. Mama is dragging Father Timothy along. If she can drown you in champagne, she wants someone there to tie the knot."

"Arrrrgh! That woman has no boundaries!"

"That's what I said!" Maria had commandeered Rocco's phone. "Your mothers are outrageous. I figured you'd want to know."

"Thanks, Maria. You're a good friend."

"Here's your brother."

"Yo," Rocco said.

"Seriously, Bro. You weren't going to tell me?"

"I hadn't decided."

I laughed. "I'm calling about Captain Bob."

"What's up?"

"He's in a shitload of trouble."

"Where are you?"

"At home."

"I'll be there in five minutes."

I was dressed in three and Rocco made it in four. The kettle whistled in five. I ground coffee beans and made a pot of French press.

Rocco's head popped out of the fridge. He found Mama's cannoli and the last droplets of half 'n' half.

"Your cupboards are bare, Sis. I depend on you to stock junk food. You know Maria won't let a Cheeto darken our door."

"I need to go shopping."

"Buy Cheetos."

I scratched Cheetos on a long list on the fridge and Rocco added Fruit Loops and Cracker Jacks.

"What are you?" I said. "Eight?"

"Forget it." Rocco dragged the list from the fridge and pocketed it. "I don't trust you with my Fruit Loops. I'm giving this list to Jackson. He'll drop your food off today."

Jackson is Rocco's partner. He's single and he loves food almost as much as he loves women.

"Jackson won't mind?"

"Not at all. You hate going to the grocery store and Jackson hangs out there. He says he meets his best dates in the produce department. Particularly around the cucumbers and tomatoes."

"That's not creepy at all."

Rocco laughed.

I signed a blank check for the groceries. "Tell Jackson to add a case of beer and some juicy steaks for himself. And I don't want him squeezing my tomatoes."

"My partner is a guy. I'm making no promises."

We carried our coffees and cannoli into the living room. I told Rocco about finding Captain Bob parked by the bakery, skulking in his car.

"He was skulking?"

"He didn't want to be seen. He was watching the live feed of Sammy."

"Why there?"

"Huh?"

"Why was the Captain parked on that block?"

"I dunno. Maybe he was driving and pulled over to make a call."

"Maybe."

I knew he didn't believe it.

"Sammy wants to come home. He's scared." Inga climbed on my lap and watched me with soulful eyes. "Who could do such a terrible thing?"

"And why? What do they want?"

"They haven't made demands yet. But I get the feeling Bob knows what this is about."

Rocco dragged out his cell. "It's about September 19, 1999. When we know what happened that day, we'll have a list of possible suspects. One of those meatheads will have Sammy."

He punched a number and put the phone on speaker.

"Rocco!" Papa said. "Come on down to Mickey's. Your Uncle Rudy will buy you a beer."

Mickey's is a cop bar and if you wear a shield, everybody knows your name. It's a hangout for the good men and women of the Ninth. The food is good and the drinks are strong. And if you like cops, you'll enjoy the company.

"Maybe later. I'm kind of into something. I'm hoping you can help."

"Name it."

"September 19, 1999. You and Bob were partners. What happened that day?"

Silence.

"Papa? Are you there?"

"That's not your goddamn business."

Click.

"Papa?"

Rocco turned to me, stunned. "He hung up on me."

I took the last bite of my cannoli and licked my fingers. "He can hang up but he can't hide. We know where he lives."

Rocco's mouth hardened to a thin line. "I'm not waiting for him to go home. I'm hunting his ass down." He jerked his White Sox cap onto his head, stomped out of the kitchen, and slammed the front door behind him.

"Happy hunting," I said.

Inga nuzzled her head in my lap. "This will not go well," I said.

Rocco was on his way to Mickey's now. I didn't need a crystal ball to see a train wreck. My brother would demand answers from Papa. They would butt heads. And a whole bar-full of cops would slowly rise to their feet.

Rocco might have the respect of his fellow officers. But Tony DeLuca is a hero. He was struck down on the mean streets of Chicago. And he's not above playing the wounded warrior card. The moment Rocco raises his voice, every cop at Mickey's will line up behind Papa.

I looked at Inga. "Meet me in the office, partner. We need a backup plan."

◇◇◇

Before Rocco could drive to Mickey's and make an ass of himself, I knew what Papa didn't want to tell us. What I didn't know was why.

It wasn't rocket science. I Googled the *Chicago Sun-Times* Archives. The *Times* is a morning paper so I brought up the following day's edition. September 20, 1999. I keyed in the words: Bridgeport, police, DeLuca, Maxfield. Two articles flashed on my screen.

The first piece reported a hit-and-run incident involving a beloved Bridgeport man the previous day. According to witnesses, Daniel Baumgarten was attempting to cross the street outside his jewelry store when he was struck down by a white van. He was hospitalized in critical condition. The identity of the hit-and-run driver was not immediately known. The Chicago Police requested anyone with information to contact Officers Antonio DeLuca or Robert Maxfield at the Ninth Precinct.

The next article revered Daniel Baumgarten as a generous man known for his dry humor and wit. The staff writer went in-depth about the jeweler's background and contribution to the community.

A second paragraph detailed his training in Amsterdam's Gassan Dam Square and his distinctive and creative use of colored stones. The writer included a photograph of the governor's wife at the inauguration ball wearing an original Baumgarten diamond-and-ruby brooch. She appeared considerably happier than she would a few years later after her husband was indicted on corruption charges.

I pressed *Print* and glanced at my watch. It was almost twelve-thirty and Sophie would be here at two. Captain Bob had hijacked her lemon tart so I plated two pieces of Tino's tiramisu. I was putting them in the fridge when Rocco swept in and snatched one from my hand.

"Fork," he said.

I handed him one. "Did you see Papa?"

"I did."

"Did he tell you about that day in September?"

"He didn't."

"So what did he say?"

"He said I'm a horrible son."

"Ouch."

Rocco winced. "I've never seen him wound up like this. He stood up and grabbed his scar like I'd shot him a second time."

"Holy crap."

"It gets better. A bunch of my cop 'friends,'" Rocco made air-quotes here, "jumped to their feet, like they would wrestle me to the ground for abusing a helpless, old man. Uncle Rudy called them off."

"Everybody loves Papa. He's a local hero."

"Shut up."

I waved the *Chicago Sun-Times* articles in his face. I couldn't swallow my grin. It was a stickler.

"I found it, Bro. September 19, 1999. There was a hit-and-run in Bridgeport. Officers Antonio DeLuca and Brian Maxfield were the first responders."

"What about the victim?"

"Daniel Baumgarten. Owner of Baumgarten Jewelry."

"That's where you found Bob sitting in his car."

"Skulking in his car."

"Do we know who drove the vehicle?"

I shook my head. "I didn't look for later articles. But I'm willing to bet that the person who took Sammy has a connection to the hit-and-run."

"I'll slip over to Records and pick up the file. Then we can begin drawing up a list of possible suspects."

"Something terrible happened on the street that day. Something Papa and Bob kept secret all these years. What could be so awful that neither will talk about it?"

Rocco was still pissed. "Papa could've said there was a hit-and-run. It's no big secret. It was in the *Tribune*."

"Probably. I got this from the *Sun-Times*."

"Whatever."

"Sometimes you have to schmooze Papa." I whipped out my cell and called his number. When he picked up, I heard laughing in the background. Good times at Mickey's.

I put the phone on speaker.

"Caterina," Papa said. "Come join your Uncle Rudy and me."

"Where are you?"

"Hanging out at Mickey's. Your brother came by all full of himself."

I feigned shock. "Not Rocco!"

He grunted.

"I love you, Papa."

"*Ti voglio bene anch'io,*" he said softly.

"So when Rocco asked you about September 1999, did you think about the hit-and-run on West 35th?"

Papa's surprise translated to an audible choke.

Click.

I smiled at Rocco. "That's a big yes, Bro."

Chapter Five

When the doorbell rang at 1:58, I was in Margaritaville, squeezing limes and humming Jimmy Buffet. Sophia was perfectly punctual, as always. And perfectly gorgeous. My sister is a clone of Barbie.

I carried two margaritas to the living room and took a good swill of mine before placing both on the coffee table. I opened the door and my smile quickly warped into a chimpanzee's grin of fear.

Sophie stepped inside and she wasn't alone. A reckless gang of devil children shadowed her. One wrangled free and made a dive for the Chihuly vase on the hallway table. I caught his collar and gently wrestled him and his mama and her demolition bandits onto the porch. I firmly closed the door behind me.

"My babysitter bailed on me," Sophie said. "Is it okay if the kids play in your yard?"

"Yay!" they yelled.

"Can you promise you won't tie the beagle's tail in a knot again?" Sophie said.

"Promise!" They screeched.

They were lying. I know this because I saw their little tail-tying fingers twitch.

"Of course they can play here. But what are grandmas for?"

"Nonna! Nonna!" the devil children chanted.

I whipped out my cell and Mama picked up on the first ring.

"Sophie's babysitter couldn't make it. The kids are at my house."

Mama caught her breath. "You know better than to bring my angels into that dangerous place. There are sharp glass edges and electrical outlets everywhere."

"It's a war zone, Mama."

"I'm on my way! And watch Inga's tail."

"Hurry. Your grand-dog is quivering behind the couch."

Mama's Ford Fusion screeched to the curb as Sophie buckled the last child into his car seat.

"My angels! *Miei bellissimi angeli,*" she sang and her face shone. Mama's heart never has gas when she's with her grandkids. She took the kids to her house, vowing ice cream on the way. She left the keys to her Ford with my sister. If I were Sophie, I'd take Mama's car and make a run for the border.

"Your tail is safe!" I called and Inga crept out from behind the couch.

Sophia gave her giddy laugh. "The children love animals. We should get them a puppy."

"Please don't."

"So why did you want to see me?"

I had the stupid look on my face.

She frowned. "That's what Mama said."

"I did!" It was coming back to me now. "I wanted to catch up. You didn't seem like yourself last time we talked."

"How did I seem?"

"I dunno. Less perky."

Sophie plopped on the sofa and rested her head back on the cushion. I grabbed the margaritas and sat beside her. She threw her head back and downed hers in a gulp.

"No brain-freeze," I said. "Impressive."

"My head is in excruciating pain. But after childbirth…"

She let the sentence hang and I made a mental note to adopt.

She blew a big sigh. "I adore my kids. They're sweet. They're fun…."

I bit my tongue. Inga shuddered.

"But lately I've been feeling, I dunno. Like I've lost *me* along the way."

"I get that."

"No you don't." She sounded bitter. "Your life is a big, selfish Cat party. You have no responsibilities."

"I have a business and a mortgage. And a partner who eats a lot of expensive sausages."

She dismissed my woes with a wave of her hand. "You date *lots* of guys."

She said it with a mixture of disgust and admiration.

"You travel and you get to have adventures. Nobody needs you or loves you so much. They don't hang on your skirt twenty-four bloody hours a day."

I bit my tongue and tossed down my drink. Instant brain freeze.

"It's not fair," she whimpered. "My life is totally, utterly predictable. Peter is the only guy I've ever kissed."

Euuww.

I massaged my frozen brain.

"I've never been outside the U.S. and with the kids' college fund, that's not going to happen." She gave a wistful sigh. "And Max is…."

"Max?"

Her face took on a dreamy glow. "It's a fantasy, I know. But he's so deliciously hot and hunky. When I danced with him at your thirtieth and at Mama and Papa's wedding…his arms were around me and…" Her face flushed. "I think about him a lot."

"Holy crap."

I pulled two fresh margarita glasses from the cupboard and salted the rims. Then I filled each glass to the top and stuffed one in her hand.

She giggled and tossed it down, absorbing another brain freeze without a flinch.

"Even when I'm in bed with Peter, I…."

I shoved my glass aside and grabbed the bottle of tequila. I chugged a long pull of my good friend Jose.

When I looked at her again, Jose and I were smiling. I slapped an arm around her shoulder. "Tell me, Sophie, what is it that you want?"

She threw me a secretive, wicked smile. "Just once, I want to be reckless like you. I want an adventure. And for the first time in my life, I want something juicy to spill at confession."

That sounded reasonable enough. "Then you should have an adventure."

She clapped her hands. "Mama said Cleo is out of town this week."

"Until Tuesday night. Her sister's getting married."

Her eyes widened. "Her sister the nun?"

"No. Her sister the ho."

Sophie giggled. "I thought there was one Sister. Get it?"

"I got it." It wasn't that funny. "There are two sisters. The ho ran off with Cleo's husband, Walter."

"Cleo should've killed him."

"Someone beat her to it."

"At least she tried."

"Yeah."

"That's cool. I guess Cleo forgave her sister. I mean she's going to her wedding."

"Her sister's marrying a sleazy guy whose pants drop at the scent of a woman. I almost feel sorry for the ho. She's in for some misery."

"Why doesn't Cleo warn her?"

"Cleo thought about it. But she decided to dance at her wedding instead."

My assistant, Cleo Jones, is smart and capable. She's a kick to work with. She's also super high maintenance. Her eyes get disturbingly glossy when she handles a gun. Hoping she doesn't shoot someone can be exhausting.

As much as I adore Cleo, I was loving every minute she was away. I needed this break. Cleo wasn't the only one doing the happy dance.

"You should know I don't shoot people," Sophie said soberly.

"Good to know."

"If there's shooting involved, you'll need to do it. I have boundaries."

"Hold on. Huh?"

"I'd like a badge or a silver star. If I'm going to be a real detective for a week, I need leverage. And I don't expect you to pay me as much as you pay Cleo."

I choked. "What?"

"Because I won't have to hire a sitter. Mama will watch the kids. It was her idea."

"Stop there. Mama has terrible ideas."

She laughed and clapped her hands. "I'm taking Cleo's place when she's away."

"Whoa! I don't…"

"This is my first real job since working at the St. Peter's Books & Gifts before the kids were born." She gave a sly smile. "I want Max to train me."

"Another bad idea."

She giggled. "This will be fun like when…"

"Like when you wrote *Cat loves Billy* on my locker and the principal dragged me into his office?"

Her laugh was a giddy trill.

My fingers flexed. I could still feel them around Barbie's throat.

◇◇◇

I watched Sophie drive away toward Mama's house. She was on her way to pick up the devil children. I would've hauled ass the other way.

My nosy neighbor, Mrs. Pickins, peered through her curtains. For once, I didn't wave. I'd had my quota of crazy.

My cell phone vibrated and Savino's number came up. "Hey, Babe," I said.

"What's good for takeout? Thai or sushi?"

"Indian."

"White or red?"

"I have both. Uncle Joey found some Michele Chiarlo that fell off the back of a truck."

"At a truck stop in Superior, I believe. There was a bulletin last week. The agents working these truck hijackings are seriously after these guys."

My voice iced. "So, Special Agent In Charge Savino. Are you going to interrogate my uncle about it?"

He laughed. "If there's no bloodshed, I don't mess with family. But I'll take a bottle of the red."

"Would that be considered hush money then?"

"Definitely. In fact I'll take two. And you might want to give Joey a heads-up."

My head hurt. I rubbed it. "Noted."

"Something's wrong, Babe. What's up?"

"My switched-at-birth sister just left."

"I wasn't sure she knew where you lived."

"Mama's got a big mouth. She told Sophie she could take over for Cleo while she's away for the wedding."

"Sorry, Hon. Your mama is sneaky and has mastered getting her own way."

"No sneakier than yours. The two are in cahoots."

He groaned. "This can't be good."

"Understatement! They sabotaged our anniversary. You're an only child, for chrissake. How can you have so many relatives?"

"My relatives live far, far away."

"Well they're all coming to Chicago."

Chance muttered a few choice words under his breath. He rarely swears. Apparently learning his family is coming to town is one of those occasions.

"Tell me about it tonight. And don't worry. I got this."

"You'll take care of our mothers?" I sounded doubtful.

"Yes. And don't stress about Sophia. You can do this."

"I'm not sure. What if I need an alibi?"

"I got your back."

◇◇◇

I didn't know how long I'd been sleeping when I was awakened by the rustle of a plastic bag and the smell of Cheetos in my face. "Go away," I said not opening my eyes.

Rocco gave my hammock a push and the rocking almost lulled me back to sleep.

"I'm dropping off Jackson's groceries. Four big bags. Come inside. I gotta have a bowl of Cocoa Puffs."

"Mmm. Cocoa Puffs?"

"I added a few items to your list."

I shook off my nap and tagged along inside.

"Did you get the case file for the hit-and-run?"

Rocco shook his head grimly. "Captain Bob checked the file out this morning. It was a cold case."

"So the driver of the white van was never apprehended. Do you think someone blames Captain Bob for that?"

Rocco shrugged and splashed milk on his Cocoa Puffs. "We won't know anything until we get a look at that file."

I began putting away groceries. "I've been thinking about the guys who took Sam I Am."

"They have to be insane to go after a police captain. Or they're desperate. Or they have a death wish. I mean Captain Bob has the entire CPD behind him."

"Only he didn't. They knew he wouldn't round up the troops. Why is that? What is so terrible that Captain Bob and Papa couldn't tell anyone?"

Rocco didn't like where this was going. "Papa and Captain Bob are the most straight-up cops on the Chicago Police force. They do everything by the book."

"On September 19th, 1999, they didn't."

"Don't." Rocco was angry.

"All I'm saying is there's a reason that Papa and Bob won't talk about that day. Something happened. We're going to find out what it is. And when we do, it's not going to change who they are or what we know to be true about them."

It bothered Rocco to think Papa had a secret. Me, not so much. I figure everyone's got something. Maybe a secret they're ashamed of or something so deeply personal they'd just as well take to the grave. Right now it seemed Papa and Bob wouldn't have that luxury.

"We need to get that file," I said.

"No shit, Sherlock."

"Is this a stakeout? Is Captain Bob helping you?"

"Are you stalking me, Sophie?"

"I'm a detective, aren't I?"

She had a point.

"Did you get my badge yet?"

"You realize you left my house a few hours ago."

"Oh. Bummer."

"Go home, Sophie. You don't want to be here."

"Oh, yes I do."

"No, ya don't." I took a deep breath. "I'm breaking into Captain Bob's house."

"How exciting! Does Bob know?"

"Of course Bob doesn't know. That's the definition of 'breaking in.' It can get you a nickel in the clink."

Her eyes widened and for a moment I thought she'd bolt. But she surprised me.

"I guess we'll be roomies then."

I grabbed her arm. "Walk."

We walked around the block before cutting through the alley and barreling over Captain Bob's fence. My eyes scanned the backyard. The front gate on the left side of the house would be where the monsters got Sammy. It had been a risky move and in full view of the street. But it was the only place where a dog could be lifted over the fence and scurried away.

Sammy, like Inga, is a trusting soul. A piece of bacon would seal their fates.

Sophie played lookout while I negotiated the back door. It had a deadlock with a combination and cracking it ate up precious time. But it was no contest for this hotshot PI. I did my magic and pushed Sophie inside before closing the door behind us.

Sophie's eyes were shining. "I want to do that."

I didn't remind her that I tried to show her a hundred times when we were kids. Papa and his brothers were teaching me to pick locks when Sophie was force-feeding her dolls.

Sophie had a sudden thought. She gasped. "Is Captain Bob sleeping around? Is that why we're snooping in his house?"

"The only thing Bob hides from Peggy are his lemon crème donuts."

I moved through the kitchen, the dining room and to the living room closet. Lots of coats, shoes, and a blue-and-white-striped leash for Sammy. No black leather briefcase.

I checked Ellie's old bedroom. She and I spent hours there reading Nancy Drew and mastering *Super Mario*. The four-poster bed was gone now. Ken's remodeling had transformed the small room into an airy office with warm earth tones, intending to lower Bob's raging blood pressure. I rummaged through the desk drawers and a file cabinet by the door. Nada 1999.

I think I felt a breeze move through the house before my mind registered the squeaking noise. It sounded like it came from the upstairs bathroom window. That squeaky window was Ellie's escape route in high school; out the window and down the old oak tree. And back through the squeaky window before dawn.

Sophie's eyes widened with panic. She ran into the kitchen for a weapon. There were knives. A meat cleaver. A cast iron skillet.

She grabbed a wooden spoon.

Oh, Barbie.

I motioned to Sophie. She followed me to the living room and behind the staircase where Ellie and I liked to hide when we were kids. It was smaller than I remembered, but so were we. I shoved Sophie inside and tapped an index finger on my lip. Then I closed the door and pressed my back against the wall.

I waited for the dog snatcher to descend the stairs.

I heard movement. Doors and drawers opening and closing. He was searching for something and it could have something to do with Bob and Papa's secret. I tucked the stun gun back in my pants. Sam I Am was my first priority. I would stay out of sight and follow this asshole. He'd lead me to him.

Maybe I'd rescue Sammy and wave to Bob on live feed. Then I'd frame a picture for his office.

I reached in my pocket and dragged out my phone and hit the video record.

"Say cheese," I whispered.

The dog snatcher slid silently down the steps. I craned my head back and videotaped his, er, make that *her* descent.

The dog snatcher was a woman dressed in burglar-Babe black. We wore the same purple latex gloves. She had long, honey-blond hair and aquamarine eyes. The diamonds in her ears tugged at my brain. But the necklace rang my memory bell.

It was the skulker outside Baumgarten's Jewelry. The woman in green. The thief. This morning she'd been a redhead. But the wig and the green scarf were gone.

She was athletic and strong but I had three inches on her. And unless she grew up wrestling three brothers with Ninja Turtle combat techniques, I could take her down.

Besides, I had a stun gun.

I was well hidden in this dark corner behind the stairs, and unless she turned and looked deliberately my way, I was safe. I remembered her piercing aquamarine eyes in the jewelry store window. They saw me. They saw everything. I tucked my phone away and reached for the taser behind my back.

That's when my switched-at-birth sister, stuffed in the dusty closet beneath the stairs, sneezed.

The dog snatcher twisted around and her eyes held mine. In a millisecond, they registered recognition. Impressive. It took me two earrings and a stolen necklace to make the connection. But then, I didn't throw her off with a dodgy disguise.

She saw me reach for the taser behind my back and she lunged at me. She threw herself on me as if she grew up with bloodthirsty wolves. I fought back and knocked her to her knees with my mad Ninja Turtle skills. I grabbed at her and she escaped my grasp as if diffusing to thin air. I held a necklace and a fistful of honey-blond in my hand.

"What do you want with Captain Bob?" I said.

"Your captain has something that belongs to my pops. Now I

have something that belongs to him." She smirked. "Even trade. We can end this now."

"There must be some kind of misunderstanding. Bob's an honorable guy. He's the most straight-up cop I know."

She gave a bitter hoot. "He and his partner stole a medallion from a dead man. How honorable is that?"

I couldn't have been more stunned if she'd slapped me. She looked at me and our eyes locked.

"You're wrong. Papa is not a thief."

"My pops may be a thief. But he's not a liar."

She didn't flinch and I knew she was telling the truth. At least she believed she was. Her eyes darted toward the kitchen door. She was calculating making a run for it.

"Not so fast. Are you talking about the hit-and-run victim? What's this medallion your dad said they took?"

She gave a hard laugh. "Ask your old man. I doubt he'll give up his bullshit lies."

"Nobody calls my papa a liar."

A hell-bent fury unleashed deep inside me and I was fueled by an anger that would, at another time, scare the crap out of me. I hurled myself at her, clawing, and pushing her to the ground. I pounced on top of her, straddling her and holding her arms down with my hands.

The closet door swung open and Sophie's terrified face emerged, eyes squeezed shut, screeching like a banshee. The wooden spoon was history. She wielded an aluminum baseball bat in her hands, swinging blindly.

"No!" I screamed but it was too late. A shattering pain scrambled my brain and I was aswim in a galaxy of stars.

Chapter Seven

I came to consciousness reluctantly, unwilling to open my eyes. The pounding in my skull was paralyzing. I tried to touch my head but my hands were cuffed behind me. My ankles seemed to be tied in a knot.

"She's gone," Sophie said in a hoarse whisper. "I scared her off."

I opened one eye. "You scared her after she tied us up?"

"She's a raging bitch."

"What happened?"

"I guess she knocked you out, huh?"

I opened the other eye. "You know I'm going to have to kill you."

Sophie's lip trembled and her eyes welled. "I was scared. It was dark. I dropped the wooden spoon."

And she found an aluminum bat.

"Sophie," I said more gently, "next time, please stay in the closet."

"Hmmm."

It wasn't exactly a commitment.

"And when you come out, open your eyes."

"You're not going to fire me?"

I shook my head and something sounded like loose marbles. This was going to be the longest week of my life.

I slid my hands down over my bum and stepped through the cuffs. *Voila*! My hands were in front of me.

"Wow," Sophie said. "I want Max to teach me to do that."

I threw her a look and "I Adore Mi Amor" blasted from my front pocket. It was Chance. My fingers grappled the phone. I zipped a finger across the screen and punched speaker.

"Hey, Babe," I said. "Where are you?"

"At your house. Your Indian dinner is hot. The wine is breathing. And I'm defending the curry chicken. Are you on your way? I don't know how much longer I can hold Inga off."

"There's been a complication. I'm tied up here."

"Can I help?"

"Not unless you pick Captain Bob's lock like I did. It's a deadlock with a combination."

I heard him smile. "You make me proud, Babe. What's tying you up?"

"Zip ties."

His growl sounded dangerous. "The captain tied you up?"

"That was the burglar."

"You followed a prowler into the house?" Savino bit his tongue and winced rather than call me an idiot. I figure if he hangs in there with me long enough, his tongue will be hamburger.

"The prowler came later. Captain Bob isn't home yet."

"I'm on my way. I may not be able to crack a combination-deadbolt but I can shoot my way in."

"Hold on, Rambo. Bob will be home soon. He hasn't gone to bed past ten in twenty years. Besides, if you charge in here, guns blazing, who's going to bail us both out? You're my one phone call."

"Do you know a sleazy lawyer with a get-out-of-jail-free card?"

"Call Uncle Joey. He's got a card for everything."

Savino has an astonishing capacity for self-control that's totally missing from the DeLuca gene pool. I suspect it comes from being raised by pot-smoking hippies.

"I love you," he said unexpectedly.

"Ditto. Don't worry. This is a hiccup. I'm not dying."

"You dance that fine line, Babe."

"Have a glass of wine and guard the chicken. I'll be home as soon as I can."

Click.

"He loves you," Sophie said. She didn't have to sound so astonished.

I pushed two buttons for my second call. Mama has Father Timothy on speed dial. I have a man who's always itching to arrest me.

"Captain Maxfield." Bob's voice was a soft roar.

"Bob," I said.

Click.

I speed-dialed again. I was mildly surprised when he answered.

"Don't hang up," I said before Captain Bob could speak.

"Go away."

"I'm afraid I can't do that. I'm a bit tied up. I'm in your house."

His voice became menacing. If we weren't such good friends, it would've been scary.

"You're. In. My. House?"

"There's no need to thank me, Bobby. You were the victim of a prowler. I've secured the premises."

"What prowler?"

"A heartless dog-napper, Captain. We followed her in and we scared her away."

Captain Bob sputtered.

"Help!" my sister screeched. "We're lucky to be alive."

"Sophia? My God, Caterina. What have you dragged your sister into?"

"She wanted an adventure."

"I'm a detective," Sophie sang.

"The intruder was wearing the teardrop necklace she stole this morning from Baumgarten's."

"The perp is tall like a model," Sophie said all professional.

"Five-six, five-seven max," I countered.

"She has short, dark hair," Sophie said.

"Long, honey-blond. Flawless skin. Aquamarine eyes."

"Did she hurt you?"

"I'm fine."

"I was asking Sophie."

"Feeling the love," I said. "Please. Come home and untie us."

"I'm pulling in front of the house now."

A moment later, Captain Bob's frown darkened the doorway.

Sophie gave a little wail. He moved to her quickly and removed the zip ties from her wrists and ankles. She threw her arms around him and hugged him tightly.

"Uh, hello!" I said. "Untie me, please."

"I should have you arrested."

"Probably. But you won't. I was trying to save Sam I Am."

"You endangered your sister. She's a mother."

"She's a baby factory. And a detective," I added.

Sophie's face brightened. I've never seen her smile so big.

"What's happened to Sammy?" she said.

"Sammy's in Philly with Peggy." A vein pulsed on his temple. I waved my wrists. "Hello!"

Captain Bob took his time releasing my zip ties. Then he walked Sophie to her car.

A handful of honey-colored hair was tangled in my fingers. I scooted to the kitchen and stuffed the hair strands in a baggie. Then I scooped up the stolen diamond and sapphire teardrop necklace off the living room floor and pocketed it.

I poured two glasses of Bob's best whiskey. The bottle was a gift from Uncle Joey. His gifts have dubious origins. There are no sales receipts. Refunds and exchanges are out of the question.

When Captain Bob returned he sat on the couch and opened his laptop. Sammy's woeful eyes filled the screen. I brought his whiskey and sat next to him. He tossed the contents of his glass down his throat and took the glass from my hand. I waited for him to finish it before I spoke.

"She was upstairs, going through your drawers and closets. Who is she? What was she looking for?"

"How the hell would I know?"

"Because you and Papa responded to the hit-and-run that killed Daniel Baumgarten. September 9, 1999."

His face went red and a pulse hammered his temple. I wondered if his head would explode.

"We worked a lot of cases in 1999," he said.

"Are you seriously going there? I can't help Sammy if you won't be straight with me."

Sammy's woeful eyes on the computer screen seemed to narrow on Bob. He closed the laptop and stomped onto the back deck where he lit a cigarette. He inhaled deeply and choked a little. His lungs were protesting but not as loudly as Peggy would when she returned from her sister's. Bob gave up smoking when he and Papa were partners.

Whatever happened the day Daniel Baumgarten met his maker had been, for Bob, more horrible than I could imagine.

I stood beside him staring up at the sky. It was a moonless night and the lights of the city snuffed out the stars. He growled and killed his smoke after a few unsuccessful puffs. He'd probably restrict his self-abuse to lemon crèmes.

"You're a pain in the ass, Caterina."

It's true. "I know."

"I'm not going to talk about what happened that day."

Bob shuffled into the house and filled two glasses. I gulped down my whiskey before he could snatch it from my hand.

"Tell me what you can about the people who took Sammy. It might help me find him."

"How the hell am I supposed to do that? I don't know who they are or how they know what happened that day."

"They haven't contacted you?"

He shook his head. "They will. They're scum. They'll blackmail me. And when the money's gone, they'll destroy my family and my career."

He knocked back his drink and frowned at my empty glass. His face twitched.

"When I find out who these assholes are, I'll take them out."

I almost laughed. "You? Really?"

"Someone will have the stomach for it."

I felt awkward and it was hard to say. I took a deep breath and spit it out.

"Why don't you give it back?"

"What?"

"The dog snatcher said you and Papa took something off Baumgarten's body. A 'medallion' she called it. She said her dad claims it belongs to him. That's why they took Sam I Am."

"Come again?"

"They want the medallion back. That's all. When you return it, he'll give you Sammy."

He stared as if I'd lost my mind. His expression was ludicrous. And the allegation I'd made was as well.

"What the hell are you talking about?"

A heaviness lifted from my chest. Bob was genuinely mystified. What I'd always known about Papa and Bob was true. They were the two last good guys. They didn't take bribes. And they didn't steal medallions off dead men.

"What happened to you tonight?" Bob demanded. "Did you get nailed in the coconut again?"

"Yes, but…"

"Go home, Caterina. See a doctor."

Bob shuffled tiredly to the door and opened it, prepared to shove me outside.

"The man is a thief," I said.

The defeat on his face lifted and something curious burned behind his eyes. "A thief?"

I shrugged.

The door slammed. Bob crossed the room and seized my shoulders. "What else did she say?"

"Easy, Captain." I shook his hands off me.

"Tell me." He said it in a low growl.

"She said her dad doesn't lie. She's convinced he's telling the truth about this medallion. She seemed proud of him. I'm guessing he's a thief by profession. Maybe a conman or a burglar."

Bob whipped out his cell and punched some numbers. It was picked up right away.

"Tony. We've got to talk…Tonight. It can't wait…Thanks, man. I'll be here."

I plopped on the couch, smiling broadly. Papa was on his way. I would finally get some answers.

Captain Bob was grinning too. "Don't get too comfortable."

"What are you saying?"

"Leave. Now."

"You don't mean that."

"Out!"

Captain Bob was whistling when he shoved me out the door.

Chapter Eight

I drove home with my brain spinning. Something horrible happened seventeen years ago when the partners responded to a hit-and-run. Something bad enough to cause two straight-up cops to cross a line. Bob believed if their actions are exposed, even today, there would be dire consequences.

This kidnapping business seemed a comedy of errors. Bob had thought he was being blackmailed for crossing that line seventeen years ago. But the kidnappers knew nothing about Bob and Papa's secret. They had a secret of their own.

Sammy's kidnappers believed the first responders to the hit-and-run stole something off Daniel Baumgarten when he was lying on the street. Only they hadn't. And the trinket the kidnappers believed belonged to them, didn't. Because if the trinket legitimately belonged to them, they would report it to the police. And it wouldn't have taken seventeen years to pick up the phone.

I was spent when I drove home. Sophie is a bundle of ups and downs and her perpetual drama is exhausting, I needed a hot lavender bubble bath and a glass of wine. And I needed a hug.

I parked in the driveway and Chance met me at the car. He opened the door and pulled me to him and kissed my mouth. When he let me go he kissed the red marks on my wrists where I'd worked the ties. And the lump on my forehead where Sophie smacked me with the aluminum bat.

"I'm relieved Bob didn't bag you for breaking into his house. I have plans for you tonight. And they don't involve a mustached cellmate named Bertha."

"He wanted to."

Savino smiled. "Bob acts tough. But you're his best friend's kid. He went to your baptism. Your confirmation. Your..."

"High school suspension hearing."

"You're serious?"

"There was an explosion in my chemistry lab."

"You made a bomb?"

"A regrettable accident." I smiled wickedly. "I was distracted by this football jock."

"Where is he now?"

"He married my BFF, Melanie. He's enormously happy and pudgy now. He hasn't had a good run since he won the state championship with a ninety-two-yard touchdown."

"My point is you and Bob are practically family."

I rested my sore head on his shoulder. "I know. I like to remind him how much he loves me."

"Are you going to tell me why you B&E'd the captain's house?"

"Over dinner. I'm starving."

"And I want the guy who tied you up."

"Well, he's a she. She kidnapped a dog. Stole a diamond necklace. And broke into Bob's house."

"She sounds like a piece of work."

I laughed. "I almost liked her."

"She whacked you harder in the head than I thought."

"That was Sophie. She wants to be a detective."

He winced. "Sophie is dangerous enough without any weapons."

"She wants Max to train her."

"Ha! I'd pay to see that action."

"Anyway, I'm hoping you'll be able to tell me who this burglar woman is. She wore gloves, so no prints. But I have hair and a photo. You can impress me with your FBI facial-recognition technology. "

"I'll wow you with high-tech tomorrow. I plan to impress you plenty tonight."

We walked to the house. I breathed deeply the crisp Chicago air and felt better already. We waved cheerily to the neighborhood snoop and Mrs. Pickins ducked behind her curtain. I suspect Mr. Pickins rarely sees more than her back-side.

When we stepped inside, Inga barreled from the kitchen and danced around us.

"Mmm," I said. "I smell Indian food."

"That's beagle breath. She got the chicken off the counter."

I gave her my mean look. "Seriously?"

Inga's tail went wild, powered by curry chicken.

"To be fair, Inga wasn't expecting you. She overheard our phone conversation and assumed you and Bertha had plans for dinner."

"What? Bread and water?"

"There's still tandoori grilled vegetables and rice for us."

"Perfect. I brought tiramisu."

Savino's eyes rolled back in his head like Inga's and he made nummy noises. I laughed.

"And Tino made a dish he calls *pozione d'amore di Tino*. You'll love it."

"Tino's love potion?" He put a hand on my cheek and his eyes kept a soft, steady gaze. "What's in it?"

I gently bit his ear. "I have no idea. But Tino promised you'll be late for work in the morning."

Chapter Nine

The phone woke me from delicious dreams before eight. I didn't have to check the caller ID to know it was Mama. I pulled the pillow over my head until the ringing stopped. Ten seconds later the blare began again.

I smelled coffee. Glorious coffee.

"Savino," I breathed and opened my eyes. Max and Sophie grinned at me.

I snatched my sheet and yanked it up to my chin.

The hunky Special Forces guy bore six-pack abs and coffee. He was ripped and the muscles under his painted-on tee and blue jeans flexed. I dragged my eyes to his face.

My switched-at-birth sister picked up the phone and put it on speaker.

"I'm in bed, Mama," I said.

Max sat on the edge of the bed. "Good morning, Mrs. DeLuca."

I slapped him. He grinned.

"Good morning, Special Agent In Charge Savino. You're late for work."

"This is Max."

I slugged him.

"Max?"

The temperature of Mama's voice went from balmy beaches to sinking *Titanic* in zero seconds.

"Good morning, Mama," Sophie gushed. "Sleepyhead Cat is just waking up."

Everyone knows Sophie's fed, dressed, and taught the devil children to read before she left the house this morning. And she probably baked an apple pie for supper.

"Is that you, Sophie? How are my babies?"

"Fed and dressed for a zoo date with Daddy."

"What?" I said. "No apple pie for supper?"

She laughed. "An apple spice cake. The kids drew zoo animals on the frosting."

"Now she's just showing off," I said.

"So the three of you will be working together," Mama said with undisguised relief.

"Cat is leaving," Sophie said looking at me pointedly. "Max and I will be training here."

"Alone?" Mama choked.

"One on one," Sophie sang. She gaped at the testosterone practically busting out of Max's jeans. "I wanna be like Cat. You should've seen her last night. Picking locks. Kicking ass…"

Mama moaned. She must be clutching her chest.

"Sophie's joking around," I said. "Mama, take your Tums."

"Tums can't fix a broken heart."

The doctor says Mama's heart is as strong as a horse.

Mama made a clicking sound with her mouth. "Caterina, you're supposed to help your sister. She's in a fragile state."

"Gee, Mama. You might have been more specific when you gave Sophie a job at my agency."

"Don't worry about Sophia, Mrs. DeLuca," Max said. "I'll take good care of her."

Mama snorted. "Not too good, young man. My daughter is vulnerable and inexperienced and…"

"She looks like Barbie," I finished for her.

Max checked out Barbie's features appreciatively.

Sophie giggled a little. Her eyes shone. She was having her adventure.

"And stay away from my mama's secret recipe in the fridge," Mama said. "It's a highly potent aphrodisiac. I made it for Tino to give to Savino."

I groaned. "*Et tu*, Tino?"

Max grinned at me. "I didn't know Chance has trouble in that department."

"He doesn't. Mama thinks a *pozione d'amore* will rouse him to propose."

Max threw up his hands and took a step back. There was blunt terror on the tough guy's face. I cracked-up laughing.

Sophia looked momentarily confused. She's had one true love since second grade and doesn't get Max's marriage phobia.

"I'll call you later, Mama," I said. "I gotta go."

Click.

"Go," Sophie said scooting closer to Max. "Hungry?"

"I'm not eating your Mama's *pozione*."

"No," I said. "But I know who is."

I shooed them away and bounced out of bed. I pulled on sweats and a tee and trotted to the kitchen.

I wrapped up the rest of Nonna's secret recipe on a pretty plate and carried it to our neighborhood snoop's house. Mrs. Pickins answered the door warily.

"Mama made this lovely dish and suggested I bring a few pieces for you and Mr. Pickins. It's quite delicious."

She eyed the plate suspiciously, sniffing for telltale scents of arsenic.

"Mama's the best baker in South Chicago. Enjoy!"

◇◇◇

I showered and dressed in a soft lavender pullover and jeans and then I called the smartest person I know. I keep his number in my phone.

"Roger King," a familiar voice said.

Roger is a computer nerd. He and his brother own a successful software company. And unless he takes me to one of Bill and Melinda's backyard barbecues, he's probably the richest guy I'll ever know.

"Hey, Roger," I said. "Do you have a minute?"

The clipped voice suddenly oozed warmth. "Cat! How's my favorite cuz?"

I felt a big grin take over my face. Roger has that effect on people. He's genuine and kind and he's not my cousin. At least not yet. Last year Roger was a client when I introduced him to my computer-geek cousin, Ginny. They're getting married in August and their feet have yet to hit the ground.

"I'm hoping for a favor," I said.

"It's yours. Name it."

I don't usually plot a jailable felony offense over the airwaves. But I feel safe talking to Roger. He's a mega-security freak and his offices are well protected from hackers and corporate spies. He swears his phone lines are more secure than the President's.

"I'm looking for some computer magic. I need to hack into computer A, bounce a live feed from Computer B to mine, identify B's identity and hack into B's personal and financial records, as well as e-mails and contacts."

"That should be simple enough. I'm meeting with shareholders in a few minutes but I can send my number one man over."

"Is there a time you could do it? This may turn out to be nothing. But if we're opening Pandora's box, we'll have to pretend Bridgeport's sky isn't falling."

"Hmmm…" He was looking at his calendar, maybe shifting some things around. I can meet you at Pleasant House after my meeting. Is eleven too early for lunch?"

"It's perfect. Thanks, Roger."

"I'm guessing you don't want Ginny to meet us."

"I think she'd rather not know. I tell you what. Let's you and I take Ginny and Chance to The Duck Inn next week. Maybe Wednesday or Thursday. I'll wear the emerald necklace you gave me for my thirtieth birthday and we'll talk about the wedding and drink too many Manhattans and have to take a cab home."

"Not Thursday. Uh…" he remembered Ginny's instructions too late. "I guess I wasn't supposed to say that."

I groaned. "The cat's already out of the bag. Our mothers are orchestrating a lake cruise with a priest and flowers and likely a wedding cake. It's the grand sabotage."

"Don't be mad at your mama. She just wants you to be happy."

"Why are you taking her side? She scares the crap out of you, doesn't she?"

"Down to my socks." He chuckled and I could envision his round tummy shaking at this desk.

"If I'm late to the restaurant, order for me," he said. "You know what I like. And bring your computer along. The deed will be done before dessert."

Roger is not one to pass on dessert. I've seen him eat it before the entree. Especially during a thunderstorm. If Roger's struck by lightning, he's going out with a smile.

"Let there be cake," I said.

When I emerged from the bedroom, Sophie had Max in a figure four. She was sitting on him and had no intention of letting him go.

His eyes were pleading and he mouthed *Help*!

I laughed and called Inga. I blew him a kiss on my way out the door.

◇◇◇

"Is there anything I can say to make you go away?"

Captain Bob puffed up his chest and growled. He likes to think he looks scary behind his big captain's desk. I thought the powdered sugar around his mouth had a softening effect.

"I'm not talking about the hit-and-run," he said.

"That's cool."

"It is?"

"I came by to drop off your lemon crème donuts." I stood. "Good-bye, Captain."

"Sit."

I sat.

"Did you see a doctor about that hit to your head last night? Cuz you're not acting like yourself."

"Really? How does 'myself' act?"

"Pushy. Obnoxious. You stick your nose where it doesn't belong."

I shrugged. "You don't want to tell me about nine-nineteen. I trust your judgment."

"For God's sake, child. See a doctor."

I rose again to leave as running footsteps pounded the hallway. Tommy, the rookie, burst through the office door.

"Captain! Rocco's having a seizure in the break room. It looks bad. He's foaming at the mouth."

"Rocco?" My hand fluttered to my throat and the word came out as a sob.

"Stay here with her," the captain barked and barreled down the hall. The door slammed behind him.

We moved swiftly. Tommy fumbled through the desk drawers. I lunged for the captain's brown leather briefcase behind his desk. The case had a three-number combination lock. Not exactly rocket science for this hotshot detective.

I pulled a Pants On Fire Detective Agency business card from my pocket and kissed it for luck. Then I put the corner between the digits and turned one digit until I felt it catch. I did the same for the other two digits. And wha-la!

The hit-and-run file was conveniently placed on top of the pile.

"Gotcha," I said and whipped out my pocket scanner.

Tommy spread the pages on the desk and restacked them after they were scanned. It was a fat file. Photographs. Detective notes. Physical evidence. Newspaper clippings. Witness statements. Tire track analysis. It took longer than I'd thought. I could only hope Rocco was still foaming at the mouth.

We almost made it clean. I shoved the briefcase toward the floor and made a nosedive for my seat when the door shot open. The captain's beady eyes shot to the white bag on his desk. His lemon crèmes were safe.

Then they hit the brown leather briefcase. He crossed the room, firing his bad-ass look. It's a lot more convincing without powdered sugar lips.

I blurted a little sob. "How's my brother? Is he—?"

Tommy whipped a tissue from the box on Bob's desk and pressed it into my hand. I blew hard and tossed it back to him. Tommy glared at me.

Frowning, Captain Bob examined the contents of his briefcase and closed it again. This time he double-locked it with a key.

A little late, Bobbo.

He jerked his head toward the door and Tommy beat it, clutching a small, dry corner of the tissue with his fingertips.

Bob moved behind the desk and dropped in his chair. He dragged out a bottle of the finest whiskey that ever fell off the back of a truck.

He took a good swig. Everybody loves Uncle Joey.

"Your brother is fine," he announced with unmistakable relief.

"What happened?"

"Rocco choked on a piece of jerky. He was foaming at the mouth. My men stood around like pussies. I jerked Rocco off the floor and gave him a Heimlich maneuver."

I crossed to Captain Bob, threw my arms around him and kissed his cheek.

"No kisses," he growled like an eight-year-old boy. But he was busting his buttons.

"Rocco didn't want me to leave him. He was shaken up. I told him to go home, take the day off. And stay away from that beef jerky."

"That's why you eat donuts. They're better for you."

"Exactly."

I blinked back a tear. "You saved Rocco's life, Captain. You knew exactly what to do."

"That's why I'm the captain. And you're a hootchie stalker."

"Gee. I could never pull one over on you."

He chuckled. "No one does, Caterina. You know, that last clonk on your head maybe did you some good. Could've knocked some sense in you, at last."

"Wow, Bob. Just wow."

Chapter Ten

I zoomed home with the pocket scanner hot in my pocket. I wanted to make hard copies of the 1999 hit-and-run investigation and pore through them with Rocco. With a little luck we'd find a thread that would lead us to the monsters who took Sammy.

When I pulled up to the house, I could hear Max training Sophie in the backyard. My switched-at-birth sister was in Special Forces hell. Or maybe Nazi boot camp. She gasped for breath and practically begged for mercy. Max was taking no prisoners.

I felt bad for her but short of waterboarding, I wouldn't try to save her. I'd make my copies and quietly escape. Involving Sophie in Papa's hit-and-run drama was the last thing I wanted to do.

Inga and I slipped into the house and inside my office. I made two copies of the fat file and tucked them into manila envelopes. One for Rocco and one for myself. Then we tiptoed to the car.

I felt a little guilty dissing Papa this way. Maybe he and Bob had a skeleton in their closet. But then, who doesn't? Papa said this was none of our business and he was right. It wasn't. But some jerk changed the rules when he kidnapped Sam I Am. And we needed that file to find him.

Rocco and I would investigate the hit-and-run. We'd almost certainly uncover their secret and we'd do our best to keep it safe. Rocco was already finding it hard to accept the fact that Papa was shutting him out. In his mind, there's a clear, bold line that separates the good guys from the bad guys. I hoped what we found wouldn't diminish Rocco's respect for our father or tarnish their relationship. And I really, really hoped Papa would never know I filched the file.

As I walked to the car, I could hear Max and Sophie in the backyard. My sister was still groaning the boot camp blues.

My bum vibrated as I slid behind the wheel in the car. I dragged my phone from my jeans pocket and checked the name on the screen. Savino.

"Hey," I said. "Are you calling to wow me with your fancy FBI facial recognition toy? Did you get an ID on Sammy's kidnapper?"

"Sorry, Babe, we got nothin'. The hood and shadow obscured too much of the subject's face. I put a rush on the hair samples. Maybe we'll get a match."

"I hope so."

"I ran a search on Daniel Baumgartner. Did you know his shop took a hit the week before he died? A midday smash and grab."

"I didn't know that."

"Three guys with ski masks and semi-automatics smashed display cases with wrenches. It was loud. A neighboring business called it in. Thought it was gunfire."

"Were they caught?"

"They're still out there. Daniel was out of town and his son was minding the store. I saw the camera shots. He looked scared. I think he peed his pants. The guy only graduated from college a few months earlier."

"It's not something they cover in school. How big was the heist?"

"Mega. The thieves knew exactly what to take. Daniel's original pieces. All the high-end jewelry. And a dozen Rolex watches. The biggest loss was a family heirloom. Daniel often wore it under his shirt. A gold lion medallion with emerald eyes and canary yellow diamonds in its mane. It wasn't part of the store inventory and was insured separately on Daniel's home policy. Together, the insurance companies paid half a million bucks."

"That's a lot of buckaroos. Thanks, Savino."

"What about dinner? How does a papaya salad and lemongrass soup sound?"

"Like you were raised by pot-smoking hippies."

I heard him smile. "I thought I'd try some more of Tino's love potion."

"You'll have to wrestle Mr. Pickins for it."

"You gave Tino's secret aphrodisiac to your neighborhood snoop's husband?"

"Guilty."

He laughed. "I'm guessing you did it for Mrs. Pickins."

"She's damn cranky, for sure."

"You got that right."

"But it's for Mr. Pickins too. I've never seen a smile on that man's face."

"Well, I hope his is as big as mine."

"Every woman does."

I heard Sophie's voice calling from the backyard gate. "Cat? Is that you?"

"Gotta go," I said tossing the phone.

"Cat?" Sophie called.

I fired the engine and hit the gas, pretending not to hear. I could see them both run to the street in my rearview mirror. Sophie stomped her Barbie foot. Max's lips gaped open. I think he was mouthing *Help!*

◇◇◇

My favorite computer geek wore a huge smile. We were having lunch at Pleasant House and he was staring at his hot apple dumpling. It was melting his ice cream.

"When I'm happy I eat dessert first," Roger said.

I stabbed my chocolate cake with a fork. "You're the happiest guy I know."

Roger looked up from the dumpling. "I wasn't happy when I met you. You saved my life when you introduced me to Ginny."

"And I love you for making my cousin happy." I squeezed his chubby hand. "Let's see what we can do for Sammy."

Roger was true to his word. Sammy's imploring big brown eyes were up on my laptop before we finished dessert.

Roger blinked and stuffed a bite of apple in his mouth. "What do these kidnappers want? If it's money, I'll pay it."

"Unfortunately, they want a rare piece of jewelry that Bob doesn't have. He's never even seen the piece. The kidnappers don't believe him."

"Are they insane?"

"Maybe, but I don't think so. More likely they're misinformed."

Roger punched more keys and we heard voices. It sounded like a *Law and Order* rerun on the motel TV. Detective Joe Fontana was talking. A toilet flushed in the background. There was a zip and a little whimper.

A man's voice said, "You gotta piss again? C'mon. I need some smokes anyway."

The screen went black and Sam was gone.

"We have audio at least," Roger said. "The clown slapped tape over the webcam but he didn't think to disable the audio."

"Can you tell where they are?"

"I will from my computer but it might take a little time. The guy's security is like Fort Knox. Smart for a dumb ass."

"How about e-mails or social networks?"

"There's no history on the computer. It's clean. Might've bought it last week."

"The weasel probably stole it."

"I'll know if he gets careless and checks his e-mail. We'll have him."

"Thanks, Roger."

"Try to negotiate a price with these clowns. They're not getting the jewelry. In my experience, money is an equalizer. In the end, it makes everybody happy."

I smiled. Imagine that.

◇◇◇

Schaller's Pump is Chicago's oldest running tavern. Since 1881, its walls have been privy to a multitude of delicious secrets and sins. The Pump ran a horse-booking operation for decades. It was a Prohibition speakeasy, a second office for five Chicago mayors who hailed from Bridgeport.

I called Rocco and asked him to meet me there. We had a few secrets of our own.

I found a quiet spot in the back and slapped the copies of the file from Captain Bob's briefcase on the table. We drank a pitcher of beer and Rocco, who never turns down food someone else pays for, gnawed on a butt sandwich. It's a house favorite.

The hit-and-run investigation had been thorough. Daniel Baumgarten had been well liked and his death was emotionally charged for the community. Witnesses were interviewed at the scene and some were questioned a second time. While fleeing the scene, the driver sideswiped a parked car. Samples of glass and paint were collected and forensics were able to identify the make and model of the vehicle that ran down the jeweler. The good citizens of Chicago were urged to report a white ninety-six or ninety-seven Chevrolet SUV with recent damage or repair to the right front bumper.

My brother kicked his chair back. "If there's a smoking gun here, I'm not seeing it."

I nodded. "What I don't get is why Daniel was in the street. Was there something he was running to? Or from?"

"Hit-and-runs are usually less sinister. The guy could've been preoccupied. Had a lot on his mind."

"The witnesses agree the hit was unavoidable. The hit-and-run driver should've turned himself in. Maybe get a fine and suspended sentence." I stole one of my brother's fries. "I wonder why he didn't."

"Cuz he's a coward. And maybe he was drunk. Or driving under a suspended license. Could've had warrants. No insurance. Or all of the above."

"Maybe he had a mistress in the car."

Rocco grinned. "You're such a hootchie stalker."

"Savino learned there was a major heist at Baumgarten's a week before the hit-and-run. It's surprising the robbery isn't in the file."

"Not if the investigators concluded that the events were unrelated."

"How could they know that for sure? Daniel Baumgarten could've been depressed after the robbery."

"And he ran into the street deliberately? You're suggesting suicide?"

"Not suggesting. Just sayin'. It's odd behavior."

"Yeah."

"What happened to Daniel's shop? Was it sold?"

"It went to Daniel's son, Robert. He had a business degree from Harvard. He expanded after his father died. He has branches in Glenview and Wheaton. And he operates an online store."

"I'm impressed you know this."

"Google is my friend. I stayed up late."

"Did you learn anything else?"

"I learned I'm not doing that again. Maria didn't wait up for me. She wasn't happy."

I laughed. "Do you have time for another short stop before you go home and make it up to her?"

"Where are we headed?"

"Baumgarten's. We've got questions. And if Daniel's son is as smart as you say, he'll have some answers."

Chapter Eleven

Robert Baumgarten was trying to close a sale when Rocco and I sailed into Baumgarten Jewelry. A half-dozen sparkling diamonds on a soft black velvet cloth almost danced under special fluorescent bulbs. The romantic background music could've had subliminal "buy buy buy" messages behind the saxophone. The bride-to-be sighed happily. She was buying it. The groom, not so much.

"Here!" she said. "I want this one!"

Her perfectly manicured finger pointed to the biggest, dazzling diamond on the black velvet cloth. It was a showstopper and it made my eyes pop.

The jeweler's lips spread ear to ear.

The bride swept her long blond hair from her face. She went *blink blink* at the groom.

"Okay, Baby?"

He looked scruffy, as if she'd dragged him away from his job at the car wash to pick out a ring.

"I told you, Babe. I got your diamond here. We want this guy to make a new ring with it."

He waved a diamond ring in her face. Her eyes went cold but she worked her full Botox-infused lips into an adorable pout.

"I want my own diamond."

His face twitched a little. "It's your diamond now."

"That's your mama's ring. Or so you *say*," she added.

Rocco and I exchanged glances. It seemed likely the guy found a cheap ring at a pawn shop. Or even cheaper in a burglary.

The groom's fist slammed the display case.

The jeweler winced. "That's glass."

"Take it," the groom said. "My mother yanked this ring off her finger when dad ran off with the nanny."

"I won't wear it. That ring is cursed. Diamonds absorb negative energy." She turned to the jeweler. "Isn't that right?"

He gave a little nod and shrugged apologetically to the groom. "Good and bad energy, actually."

"And your mama's energy ain't good," she said.

"What did you say?"

"I said, Your. Mother. Is. A. Witch."

Holy crap, I thought.

His voice became terrifyingly quiet. "Take. It. Back."

"Witch! Witch!"

He lunged at her, seizing her shoulders and shaking her like a rag doll. Rocco dragged him off her and over to a table where contracts are signed. It was the only surface that wasn't glass. He shoved him on a chair and flashed a badge. The groom's lip curled and his eyes grew sullen.

But I saw fear in the bride's.

Rocco took a step toward the sulky groom. "Don't make me arrest you for being stupid. The lady doesn't want the ring."

He growled. "Okay. I got it, already." He knocked his head toward the door. "We're outta here, Babe."

Rocco stepped aside.

"Wait. Not so fast," I said. "Botox here needs to empty her pockets."

The jeweler glanced down at the velvet black cloth and gasped. "My diamonds!"

"Yeah," I said. "Bonnie here palmed them when Clyde threw her against the case."

She hurled hate-darts with her eyes. "Bee-itch!"

She stuffed a hand in a pocket and tossed the rocks back on the counter. She turned suddenly and made a dash for the door.

The jeweler scooped them up and kicked something with his shoe. A loud, metallic sound resonated from the door.

"We're locked in," Robert Baumgarten said. "The cops are on their way."

And then he began locking all the glass cages as if cops posed the greatest threat of all.

"Isn't this cozy?" Rocco smiled and dragged out the handcuffs.

My Cousin Frankie was the first responder. He charged into Baumgarten's with a hand on his holster, ready to shoot somebody. His eyes take on a disturbing glaze when he handles a gun. It's one reason why the FBI turned down his application. There were many.

Luckily for Frankie, an eagerness to shoot people wasn't a problem for the Chicago PD. They gave him a badge and a really big gun.

Leo and the rookie Tommy arrived next. Everyone loves Leo. He's older than dirt and his joints have grown stiff. They make a good team. Tommy is young and good natured and does what Leo tells him. He chases down the bad guys. Leo surrendered the squad car keys after an unfortunate incident involving a cat, a dog, and a woman's prized magnolia tree. Only the magnolia didn't survive.

Leo dreams of retiring to Florida winters and marathon reruns of *Hill Street Blues*. Papa says he'd be out of here tomorrow if his wife wasn't home all day.

Detective Ettie Opsahl brought up the rear. Her lips almost turned up in a smile when she saw Rocco. But not enough to crack her pinched face.

And then she cast her evil eye in my direction. Ettie has a scathing contempt for private detectives in general and the Pants On Fire Detective Agency in particular. Her pants haven't seen a spark since Bill Clinton was President.

"Good work, DeLuca," she said to Rocco. "These clowns have hit a dozen south side businesses. I've been chasing them for months."

"Thank Cat," Rocco said. "She nailed your guys for you."

Ettie tried to say something but the words came out in a strangled choke. I thought her face would melt.

"You're welcome," I said.

Frankie filled out the police report. Everyone was concerned about Rocco's choking incident except Tommy. And he wasn't talking.

"Goddamn scary to see you like that," Leo said.

"Goddamn gross," Cousin Frankie said. "If you croaked like that, I'd always remember you like that. Blowing foamy bubbles. It's sick, man. I gotta purge my brain."

"What brain?" I said.

"It changes a man when he cheats death like that," Rocco said. "For a moment there, my life flashed in front of my eyes."

"You had an NDE," Leo said. "A near death experience. I'm glad you made it back."

The groom snorted. "If you hadn't, I wouldn't be sittin' here."

"You wouldn't be sitting here if you weren't a schmuck," Ettie said.

"Did you see a tunnel?" Tommy said tongue-in-cheek. "Was there a bright light?"

"The place was lit up like Christmas," Rocco said.

"Was Grandpa DeLuca there?" Frankie asked. "Is he still mad at me?"

"Choke on your own jerky and ask him," I said.

Leo dropped a heavy hand on Rocco's shoulder. "When you were over there, did they give you a message to bring back?"

Rocco nodded and the room went still. No one breathed.

"I should have more sex. And I intend to take it up with Maria."

◇◇◇

When the others had gone, Robert Baumgarten turned on his *OPEN* sign again and blew a long-suffering sigh.

"Are you still here?" he said.

"We have a few questions about the day your father died," Rocco said. "We will be brief."

"Have you found the man who killed my dad?"

"I'm afraid not," Rocco said.

"There's a suspect? New evidence?"

"Regrettably, no."

"But you're reopening the case?"

"Not yet."

Robert looked tired. "Please go away. You're wasting my time."

I butted in. "Mr. Baumgarten, we're taking a fresh look at the incident that killed your father. We've been contacted by a man who claims Daniel was in possession of the gold lion medallion when he died."

The color drained from Robert's face. "That's not possible."

"The witness insists he saw the medallion in your father's possession. Is it possible one of the thieves offered him a deal? Could Daniel have purchased the item back?"

"Ridiculous."

"It happens."

"Tell us what happened the day your father died."

"It's a question I ask myself every day. Dad never left the shop unattended. I wish I knew why he went outside or what he doing in the street. Felix got a good look at the van. He was washing windows when it happened. Dad used to give him odd jobs."

"Felix?" I said.

Rocco elbowed me hard in the ribs. He was telling me to keep my mouth shut. When Robert turned away I slugged him back. That was me telling him I'm not an idiot.

There had been no record of a "Felix" in the police report. No report of a man sweeping the sidewalk and witnessing a van hit his friend. Rocco and I were ten minutes into our first interview and we already smelled a giant cover-up.

What did this man see that was awful enough to make Papa and Bob omit evidence and falsify their accident report? Who would they risk protecting at the highest cost possible to their careers? It was no wonder Bob was frantic and Papa was chewing his nails again. Even now, if the CPD learned an officer hijacked an investigation, the facts could cost his job and his pension. And possibly criminal charges as well.

"The cops interviewed Felix a few times," Robert said. "Read your goddamn police report. The experience was painful enough without rehashing the same questions all these years later."

"I apologize, sir," I said. "Can you tell me Felix's last name?"

Robert rolled his eyes. "Proust. Felix Proust."

"An address?"

Robert snorted. "My father could tell you. I can't. Dad drove Felix home sometimes, especially in the winter when the weather was bad. Used to close the shop and take him to ballgames."

"Your dad was a good man."

Robert shrugged. "He missed almost every game of mine. Had to work those days."

"What did you play?"

Robert shot me a look. It was none of my business but he answered anyway. "Baseball and soccer."

"Rocco played soccer. He coaches his girls' teams."

The jeweler couldn't have been less interested.

"Did Felix have a car?" Rocco asked.

"Of course he didn't have a car. If you find him, you'll know why. Are you finished here? Because I am."

"Thanks for your time," Rocco said.

He turned and started for the door. I reached in my pocket and palmed the stolen jewelry the woman with the green scarf dropped on Captain Bob's floor.

"What's this?" I said. I knelt down and surfaced with the dazzling piece dangling between my fingers.

"My God," Robert breathed.

He seized the diamond-and-sapphire teardrop necklace from my hand.

"I thought I lost this. More accurately, I suspected an innocent, and very beautiful woman of ripping me off. Where did you find it?"

I smiled sweetly. "On the floor, of all places. Mr. Baumgarten, it's beyond me how you manage to stay in business."

Chapter Twelve

I was on my way home when Mama called.

"Caterina, we've been robbed."

"Oh, my God, Mama. Are you and Papa okay?"

She gave a satisfied grunt. "Ask me if the thief is okay. I chased her out of my house with an eggbeater."

DeLuca women are vicious with kitchen utensils.

"Did she take anything?"

"She didn't have the chance. She was after my silver."

"Really?"

"Some ladies would kill for it."

"What ladies?"

"Church ladies. And if you're so snooty about my silver, I'll leave it all to Sophie when I die. Very soon."

"Did you call the police?"

"I did not. Your Papa told me not to. Can you believe it?"

Actually, I could.

"Did Papa say why?"

"He said I should trust him. Last time I trusted your Papa he promised I wouldn't get pregnant. That's why we have the twins."

"Too much info."

"Talk to your Papa. He's acting *stupido!*"

I made a U-ey at the next corner. "Inga and I are on our way, Mama. We'll be there in a few minutes."

I pulled the Silver Bullet in front of Mama's house. Inga and I bypassed the front door and scooted around to the back. Papa was where I'd guessed he'd be: hovering over his fancy Viking barbecue grill, burning chicken. When Papa cooks, he likes to kill an animal all over again. Papa always cooks when he's stressed.

When he saw me, his eyeballs swam. He opened his arms wide and hugged me fiercely. I couldn't breathe.

It wasn't exactly the response I was expecting. The last time I talked to Papa, he hung up on me.

"Caterina, can you forgive me?"

"Uh, sure. What for?"

"If I'd spoken to you when you called yesterday, you wouldn't have gone to Bob's. You could have been killed. That insane woman knocked you senseless."

I didn't say the crazy head-whacker was my switched-at-birth sister.

"I'm fine, Papa. If I hadn't gone there, we wouldn't know why Sammy was taken."

He scoffed. "Medallion!"

I smiled. "And I wouldn't have impressed my sister. Sophie is training to be a detective."

"*Porca vacca!*" It takes a lot for Papa to swear in Italian.

"Do you have any idea what this 'medallion' is? This intruder's dad claims you and Bob lifted it from Baumgarten's body."

He shrugged and took a long swig of his beer. He opened the ice chest at his feet and handed me a Peroni.

He said, "Daniel Baumgarten wasn't dead on the street. He died the following day in the hospital."

"Where were you guys when you got the call?"

"We didn't. We were at the bakery across the street when the accident happened. There was a commotion outside. Some window-seat diners yelled, and Bob and I hit the floor running. We didn't miss a helluva lot. Two, three minutes tops."

"Is there anything else you can tell me?"

"It was a pretty straightforward incident. We interviewed witnesses. They said Daniel Baumgarten ran into the street without looking. The driver probably couldn't avoid the hit. If he'd hung around, he wouldn't have been charged."

It's human nature. Sometimes a flight response kicks in and a driver panics. But a person who's all grown up will eventually suck it up and turn himself in. Only this person hadn't.

Papa waved the smoke away and stabbed at the chicken. Apparently it wasn't black enough yet.

He shook his head. "Who are these asses who took Sam? And if they thought we jacked Baumgarten over a trinket on the street, why wait all this time before coming after it?"

"We'll know the answer when we bring Sammy home."

Mama emerged through the back door waving a wooden spoon. Inga ran joyfully to her Nonna, and Mama cooed and fed her a sausage. She coddled her grand-dog up a moment before standing again and shaking the spoon at Papa. He winced. A protecting hand shot to his battle scar and his eyes darted back and forth. Papa was moments away from being banished to the guest room. He tried desperately to think of something to save himself but he just doesn't think that fast.

"Did your papa tell you why I shouldn't report the silver thief?" Mama demanded.

I crossed my fingers behind my back. "He knew you were upset. He didn't want to stress you more."

"You're a foolish old man, Antonio."

"Papa made the police report for you."

"He did?"

"He went to the top of the food chain. Captain Bob's taking care of it."

Papa's astonished eyes popped. He dropped his brows when Mama looked at him. Her eyes were soft.

"L'amore fa fare cose sciocche alle persone."

He moved to her and whispered something in her ear. I guessed it was his "trust me" line. She giggled and her cheeks flushed. It seemed to be working.

"Get a room," I said and called Inga. She followed me to the car.

◇◇◇

The aroma of burnt chicken followed me to the Silver Bullet, where the hunky buns of a Nordic god kissed my Honda's lucky hood. His ripped arms folded across his chest and he rocked his blue jeans in all the right places. His skin was tanned to brown sugar and for two—okay, five—delicious seconds I wanted to lick him all over.

Don't get me wrong. I'm over-the-moon-crazy about Chance Savino. He's attentive and thoughtful and he brings me breakfast in bed. He helps with the dishes, for God's sake, and takes out the garbage without being asked. I was married to a man who didn't know where our garbage can was, much less what day I dragged it to the curb for pickup. Savino knows all these things. I don't know what other women call these household tasks. But I call them foreplay.

I looked at Max and felt my cheeks flush. My vision is twenty/twenty and Max is built like a Nordic god.

I'm not dead yet.

My mouth felt dry.

"Papa's barbecuing in back," I said.

"I can almost see the flames."

"Hungry?"

"Always. But I've had your papa's black chicken. It's carcinogenic."

I laughed. "Then we should get outta here before the fire department arrives. Wanna meet at Tino's?"

"Definitely. We'll take my car." He whistled for Inga.

Nordic gods are bossy.

"Where's your Hummer?"

"At home."

He had his hand at my back, guiding me across the street to a black Jaguar F-Type convertible with temporary plates.

"I'm showing off my new toy."

"OMG," I breathed.

Okay, I'm shallow enough to be tantalized by a hot car.

Chance Savino rocks my world. He's sizzling hot, eye candy, and utterly delicious. There's nothing I would change about him. Except maybe his car. Chance drives a boat.

When I first met him, he drove a Porsche Boxster. I thought he was super rich and smokin' hot. It turns out I was half right. Savino was working undercover when we met and the Boxster was a tease. At least he's still hot. And the cobalt blues make up for a decided lack of green.

Savino recently bought a new Prius for work but when we go out, he drives his Cadillac Eldorado with the fluffy black-and-white dice dangling from the mirror. He's as goofy and proud as a new father. He spent a year restoring the Eldorado it to its original, shiny hugeness. I suspect when he's behind the wheel, he has a James Dean alter-ego thing going. I get Ozzie and Harriet.

Max opened the Jaguar's passenger door. Inga jumped in and over the backseat. I hung my head inside and breathed in the new car smell.

"OMG," I said again and he laughed.

"Can I drive?" I said.

"Not a chance. You abandoned me with your sister."

"I—"

"Don't deny it. I caught your eyes in the rearview mirror."

"In all fairness, that woman is a stranger to me. She was switched at birth."

"That's what she said about you."

I sputtered. "Seriously? She's a foot shorter than the other kids."

He grinned. "She towers over Nonna DeLuca."

"But you told her I was the sane one, didn't you?"

"Sane? That's a bit of a stretch. Insanity runs rampant in your family."

I sputtered and he laughed.

"Actually, Sophie was amazing. She's got spunk. And courage. And an exceptional capacity to work through pain."

Of course she does. She's a baby machine.

"What she's got is a crush on you," I said.

"She's married. That's a line I don't cross. She's gorgeous, no doubt. But I keep a picture of dead puppies in my head."

"How's that working for you?"

"It works. She's your sister."

I smiled.

"And your mama scares me."

Mama scares everyone.

I climbed in the passenger seat. He closed the door behind me, scooted around the car and behind the wheel.

"How did you know I was here?" I said.

"I called Tino. He has a tracker on your car."

I made a sputtering sound but no intelligent syllables came out.

"Tino put a tracker on your Honda one of the many times someone was shooting at you. Don't get all huffy. It's to keep you safe."

"Safe from what? Papa's burnt chicken?"

"Get over it, Kitten. You piss people off."

"*Et tu*, Max?"

He laughed. "Since you're already mad, I may as well tell you I'm here because I saw the 1999 file on your computer."

"You were snooping in my office?"

"I'm a spy. But in my defense, I didn't snoop until you ran away and left us in the dust."

"Okay. I deserve that."

"I got curious. I wondered where you went in an all-fired hurry. I saw the file on the hit-and-run and I called Tino. He remembers the case well. I think we can help."

"Impossible. In 1999 Tino was probably in some exotic country doing some top secret spy stuff."

"You've watch far too many James Bond movies."

"And you?" I did the math. "I'm guessing you were in school. Or maybe Special Forces Boot Camp."

"Tino was here the end of '98 and the first half of '99. It was the year his mother was diagnosed with breast cancer. He left Eastern Europe and came home to take care of her. He hired a nurse. And at the end, Hospice came to the house. It's still painful for Tino to talk about."

I felt small. Sometimes I have a big mouth.

"I didn't know about his mama," I said.

"Tino made us dinner and there's a new wine he wants to try. And don't say you're not hungry. When your blood sugar gets low, your green eyes flash like a large, wild cat."

"Are you calling me cranky?"

"I was goin' with bitchy."

I punched him.

He laughed. "Let's say I know when to feed and water you. Sometimes I think you could eat me alive."

I dragged my eyes away from his hard muscled legs and stared out the window. I was thinking about dead kittens.

Chapter Thirteen

I was on my best behavior at Tino's. I didn't rant about Mama coercing him to pass off her *pozione d'amore* as his own. Tino is a romantic and he believes spreading some love is good for the soul.

And I didn't say anything about the tracker he put on the Silver Bullet. Tino saved my sorry bum more than once. I decided to be thankful. And to have my mechanic remove the tracker the next time he services my car.

Tino served up some delicious pumpkin tortellini in a fresh sage mascarpone cheese sauce and a warm tomato and spinach salad.

When we were finished with our plates, Max whisked them away and tidied up the kitchen.

Tino took out one of Uncle Joe's Cuban cigars and a long, fancy cedar match and began the ritual of cutting, toasting, and lighting his cigar. He took his time, slowly spinning the cigar to get an even burn and when he was satisfied, he sighed deeply before turning to me with a curious expression on his face.

"Why are you investigating Danny's death?"

My mouth dropped. "You knew him."

"I met Danny when I bought a set of wedding rings from him. Gold bands and more diamonds than I could afford." The smile didn't reach his eyes. "We became friends. His wife had died and I was here taking care of Mama. I'd cook dinner and we'd knock off a few bottles of wine and talk into the night."

Wedding rings? Had Tino been married? My head reeled but I held my tongue. I thought I should give him a chance to cough up the scoop before I choked it out of him.

"I'm sorry about your friend," I said.

"Danny had integrity. It's a rare commodity in a ball-breaking business. "

A thought came to me. "Do you remember a guy who did some manual work for Daniel? His name was Felix Proust."

"Felix. Yes. He was a good guy. Danny liked him. He could listen to him play the piano for hours."

"Do you know where he lives?"

Tino shook his head. "I'll ask around. He had some physical and mental challenges. A crooked spine, I think. Danny said he was good company."

"Rocco and I were at Baumgarten's today."

"You met Robert then. He tells me business is good."

It's the first time I'd been in the shop in forever. Peggy Maxfield took Ellie and me there when we were in school. Once she bought a watch for Bob's birthday. Another time she bought a deep purple butterfly. Wings were spread like it was flying. I forgot about it until last night. I saw it on her windowsill."

Tino flicked the ash from his cigar. "Danny and Robert had some conflict over the business. Robert was just out of school. He was young and ambitious and he wanted to maximize profits. They were both good guys. They had different visions for the business."

I took another sip of wine and pulled a leg up under me. "Okay, Tino. Spill it. Were you married or not?"

He smiled. "I was teaching English in the Russian city of Ryazan when my mama got sick."

"Drop the cover story, 007. I know you were a spy."

He gave a bark of laughter. "Such an imagination, Caterina."

"Right." I winked. "We'll play it cool."

He returned the wink. "Mama called and I came home. I was seeing a woman named Liliya but the State Department denied her Visa. She had been married a short time. Her husband was killed by the police. The police claimed he was an FSB agent and he planted a bomb." Tino gave a palms-up shrug. "The government was corrupt. Maybe he was, maybe he wasn't. But Liliya wasn't political. She wasn't a threat."

"I came home alone and petitioned the State Department to alter their decision. I called them every day for three months. The day her Visa came through, I flew back to Ryazan with the rings Danny made for us."

"I got there too late. Liliya was gone. A few days earlier, a suicide bomber drove a truck with a bomb into a crowd at the market. Nine people died. Mostly women and children. I turned around and came home again. I've never been back."

I moved around the table and hung my arms around him. He smelled of wine and garlic and cigars. I held him a long moment. When I let him go, the chocolate eyes were steady.

"I lost everything that year. My mother. My lover. My best friend."

"I'm sorry, Tino." The words sounded empty.

Tino spat. "I want you to find the *bastardo* who ran Danny down on the street. *Egli morirà!*"

A death sentence sounds scarier in Italian.

"You didn't answer my question," Tino said. "Why are you investigating Daniel Baumgarten's murder?"

"I have a client. He insists on anonymity."

"Max will work with you."

"I work alone."

Tino looked amused. "Max will see you have everything you need. Whatever your client pays, I'll double it."

"Uh, what just happened here?"

Tino smiled. "You just made more money."

Actually, I could double what Sammy was paying me all day and still not have enough to buy an ice cream.

"There's one more thing."

"I already don't like it," I said.

"Captain Bob and the Ninth Precinct. They had seventeen

years to find the guy who took Danny's life. He's mine now. I want his name. Bring it to me and walk away."

Yikes.

"Danny will have justice," Tino said. "And maybe one less ghost will hover over my bed at night."

Max emerged from the kitchen with a dish towel on his shoulder and a tray with three small glasses of Sambuca. We each took a glass and Tino held his in the air.

"To Danny. May you rest in peace."

Our glasses touched, making a soft, musical tinkle.

Max raised his glass. "To my partner."

I glared at him and he laughed.

"What's your client's name?" Tino said.

"Uh, Sam."

"Honest?"

I finger-crossed my heart.

Max grunted. "Who the hell is Sam? And why does he care about a hit-and-run every Chicago cop forgot about a long time ago?"

I gulped down my Sambuca. "Every cop didn't forget. Danny's ghost still keeps a few awake at night."

◇◇◇

I lay still and listened as Chance's breathing slowed to a deep, soft snore. When he was sufficiently zonked, I removed his hand from my hip and turned over to say good night to Sam I Am. The sleazy motel room streamed live on my laptop. Sammy was asleep in the hard, metal cage but his legs were running. He was escaping in his dreams.

"Hang in there, Sam," I whispered. "We're gonna bring you home."

I nestled my bum into the curve of Chance's body. He threw an arm around me and pulled me to him, the soft snores not missing a beat. I let myself melt into the warmth of his skin. I closed my eyes but the image didn't go away. The sleazy motel room was glued to the inside of my lids. I squeezed them tight and tried to count sheep. But the sheep's faces looked like Sam I Am and there was red sauce on his lips.

My eyes opened wide as pepperoni.

I bolted upright and seized the laptop from the nightstand. I pulled the screen to my face. I hadn't imagined it. There was a glimpse of something on the floor by the bed. I suppose it could've been anything. But it looked a helluva lot like the edge of a pizza box. And the flash of black and red was the tip of a wing.

I'd know that pizza bird anywhere.

My heart beat wildly in my chest. I slipped into a robe and dragged the laptop to my office. I magnified the image on the screen for a closer look. Then I brought up the pizzeria's website and checked their logo against the box on the motel floor. The black-and-red blob matched the tip of the dark wing perfectly.

Yes!

The pizza box came from Flying Zimbaroni's Pizzeria. The man in the motel knew they make some of the best pies that fly over Chicago. If the pizza was a delivery, I'd find out where it went. I'd do whatever it took.

I dressed quickly and silently, tugging on jeans and an oversized sweater. I pulled on socks and shoes, and was tiptoeing to the door when a groggy voice mumbled from the bed.

"Babe. Where are you going?"

"Uhm, to Flying Zimbaroni's."

"At this hour?"

"I love their pizza."

"Are you pregnant?"

His eyes were soft and he smiled as if he thought that would be a good thing.

Geesh.

I sat on the bed and kissed him. "I'm not pregnant."

He grinned. "We can try again."

He pulled me down but I squirmed away laughing. "Don't tempt me, Babe. I'm weak. And I have a lead on Sammy."

"What lead?"

"The creep in the motel bought a pizza. If it was delivered, someone's gonna tell me where."

"I'm going with you."

"You have an early meeting with the federal prosecutor. Besides, I'll be gone before you get your pants on."

"No you won't."

He threw back the covers and my mouth went dry.

"Whoa, Trigger!" I said. "Back in the barn."

Savino stomped around the room. "I can't find my pants."

I didn't remind him that I took them off in the living room.

I blew Trigger a kiss and hustled out the door. I cranked up the Silver Bullet and for the first time in memory, Mrs. Pickins' curtains didn't move.

Chapter Fourteen

The woman behind the counter at Zimbaroni's Flying Pizza had a cluster of frizzy hair as red as their sauce. She didn't want to tell me if one of their drivers delivered a pizza to a motel in the past few hours. She changed her mind when I pulled out a twenty. The answer was yes. Another twenty bought me the driver's name.

"Jared." She turned up her nose when she said it. "He drives a beat-up red Fiat."

"What motel?"

She held out her hand. I slapped a twenty in it.

"Jared is an asshole."

"I figured that out already. What motel?"

"I ain't losin' my job. You'll have to ask Jared."

"I don't suppose I can get my last twenty back."

"Not happening."

I hunkered down with Camilla Schafer and read two chapters of her newest Lexi Graves mystery while waiting for Jared to wheel into the lot. His rap music got there first. Kanye blared from his radio and the beat-up red Fiat followed. Jared took one last slow draw on his smoke before grabbing the empty thermal pizza bag and tromping toward the door.

Inga and I cut him off at the pass. We were still fifteen feet away when Jared sneezed.

He waved us away. "I'm allergic," he said.

Puh-leeze.

"One moment, Jared," I said and opened the car door for Inga. She looked over her shoulder and growled. She didn't like Jared any more than the cashier did.

I flashed a winning smile.

His uncertain eyes darted back and forth as if half expecting a subpoena or summons for some karmic behavior or unpaid debt.

"What do you want?"

"I want to pay for some information."

"How much?"

I whipped out a Benjamin. "You delivered a pizza to a motel tonight."

"So?"

His nose twitched. I had a pretty good idea what he was gonna do with it.

"I'd like to know where that pizza went and who answered the door."

He gave a disinterested shrug but his eyes never left Benny. He licked his lips.

"Privileged."

"Really?"

"It's company policy. I don't want to get fired."

"I'm discreet."

"You got another one of those?"

"I've got two." I whipped a second one out.

"Too bad. I got three kids."

"I hope not." I dragged out one more. "This better be good."

"Dreamscape Motel, room seven. One guy, about fifty."

"Anything else?"

"And a yellow dog. He had a yellow dog."

"Did he like the dog?"

"I guess. He talked to him."

"What did he say."

"Shut up, don't bark."

"Seriously? And you thought he liked him?"

"The dude was cool. He gave me a ten-dollar tip."

"Wow."

He snagged the C notes from my hand and stuffed them in his shirt pocket. His lips curled in a silly grin. I knew he was calling it quits.

"I'll be going home early." He winked at me. "I just got a killer headache."

◇◇◇

I rang the motel manager's bell three times before a sleepy-eyed clerk stumbled to the counter. He was Danny DeVito-short with big ears and a grumpy face. I was staring at two of the seven dwarves.

"Where's Happy?" I said.

He managed an even grumpier face and tapped his nametag. "I'm Bert."

I glanced at the tag. "I never trust those things."

His eyes narrowed and he looked me up and down. "You're not one of them working girls, are ya? This is a respectable establishment. I don't want no hanky-panky here."

"Your guests come for hanky-panky. It's your bread and butter. You'd be out of business without it."

His gaze settled on my breasts. I tapped the corner of my eye. "Eyes up here, please."

He dragged 'em up.

"I need a room on this end, if possible. I like the view."

"It's a street. I got rooms in back with a view of the park."

I pulled out my Sonya Olsson driver's license and Visa. Uncle Joey hooked me up with the fake ID. Grumpy looked at it. And he looked at me.

"Sonya Olsson," he read.

Grumpy had amazing reading skills.

"You don't look like a Sonya. I knew a Sonya once. She was a blue-eyed blonde."

"Wow. My uncle's name is Bert. You don't look like him at all."

He chuckled. I was mildly surprised when his face didn't crack.

"I'll take that room now," I said.

He ran my card and I signed the registration.

"Sure you don't want one of our park views? The rhodies are in bloom."

I tucked the Visa back in my bag and flashed a smile.

"It's a tempting offer, Bert. But what can I say? I'm crazy about neon."

He took a key from his desk. "Number ten," he said. "No drugs. No loud parties."

Not bad. Number ten was a few doors down from Sammy's seven.

"Eight is my lucky number," I said.

"Eight is taken."

"I like six too."

"You're a difficult woman, Ms. Olsson. The rooms are the same."

"I like six a lot."

He tossed the ten key in the drawer and held number six in the air. "Let me give you some advice."

"Do you have to?"

"If you got a secret rendezvous with number seven, I don't want to hear about it. Keep it to your lovebird selves. I don't need no jealous husband or schizo wife sniffin' 'round here raising hell."

I blinked my surprise and leaned in close. "Gee, Bert. Did you say there's a guy in seven? Is he adorable?"

He pressed the key to room number six in my hand and shuffled me out the door.

"I hope you're not staying long, Ms. Sonya. I got a bad feeling about you."

"Really? Most people have to know me a while before they say that."

He drummed his forehead. "I got the sight. I see things."

"Did you see the White Sox lose last night? Cuz I did *not* see that coming."

"You walked through the door and I got a ringing in my ears. It's still there. Do you know what it sounds like?"

"Uh, tinnitus?"

"Sirens. Sirens, and yelling, and a helluva lot of cops storming my hotel."

I studied Grumpy with unexpected interest. The guy was a goddamn psychic.

"Why am I hearing sirens, Ms. Sonya?"

Gee, I dunno. Maybe cuz you're harboring a gutter punk who's brain-dead enough to go after a CPD captain.

I flashed a smile. "Go back to bed, Mr. Bert. You're still dreaming."

◇◇◇

I let myself into number six and closed the door behind me. The room was sparse but clean and smelled of pine cleaner which, considering the options, was a good thing. I sat on the bed. It was lumpy and would do a number on a troubled back. I figured guests invested lots of quarters for a cheesy Magic Fingers massage.

The walls were thin and I could make out most of the words from a *Law and Order* rerun coming from room seven next door. A show that nails and convicts the culprit seemed a curious choice for a crook to watch. Before I left, I said a prayer for Sammy. I put a hand on the wall between us and said good night.

I parked the Silver Bullet in the motel lot with a direct view of room seven's door. I fixed a tiny spy camera to the windshield and checked the feed on my iPhone. Then I called a cab and waited on the corner for a ride home.

The text from Roger came as the cab pulled up to my house.

> Sam is at Dreamscape Motel on West Eighteenth. Be careful. Bring him home safe.

I texted back. You're my hero.

Chapter Fifteen

A searing pain in my neck woke me. I had fallen asleep at the kitchen table and had come-to in a twisted, hunched-over mess. I felt stiff in places I didn't even think about. I needed a Magic Fingers massage.

The house felt a little lonely and I knew Chance was gone before I opened my eyes. There was a soft blanket around my shoulders and he'd placed a long-stemmed red rose on the table. And he left a goofy love note under a glass of fresh squeezed OJ. I love that about him. He's got all the romance genes I lack.

Sam I Am's live image was splayed on my laptop and his sad eyes made an ache in my heart. My credit card was on the table. My tablet was open to a Central Illinois dog rescue called Holy Shih Tzu. I searched four rescues sites in the night before I found a blond bombshell Pomeranian that was a shoe-in for Sammy. Down to the white boot on his front right foot.

His name was Thor and I fell in love with him in a red hot minute. At four-thirty a.m. I paid the adoption fees with my Visa. Thor was coming home to Inga and me.

Inga pranced over with a big ol' smile on her face, ready for our morning run. She dropped her leash in my lap. I stretched my sore neck and winced.

"Sorry, girl. I gotta skip our run. I'm goin' with a hot shower."

I opened the back door and she trotted outside all snotty. She didn't glance back.

"Be nice," I called after her. "I found a grateful replacement for you on Google."

I took a long, steamy shower, letting the hot, pulsating water work on the tight muscles of my neck. I was a wet mess of bubbles when my phone rang. Usually, I'd let the call go to voice mail. But there was a good chance my wildly eccentric mechanic was on the line. Jack has made my cars purr since I was sixteen. He's a magician under the hood, but he's temperamental. And easily put off. I didn't want to piss him off again.

I fell all over myself scrambling out of the shower.

My soapy hands grabbed the phone and my voice was breathless. "Jack?"

His response was cool. "Caterina. You left a message at four a.m. Can I assume you blew up someone else's car?"

Okay. He was still pissy. Last year Jack's beloved Dorothy bit the dust on my watch. Jack's father had bought the '67 Ford Mustang straight off the assembly. It was awful. But it wasn't my fault. It's not like I planted the bomb.

I called Jack because I was without wheels. The Silver Bullet was doing surveillance at the Dreamscape Motel.

I managed a light laugh. No small feat before a flipping cup of coffee. "No bombs, Jack. Thanks for returning my call."

He grunted. "Your Accord isn't due for a tune-up until next month."

"I'm looking for wheels, Jack. I need a loaner for a day or two."

Oddly enough, Jack's been touchy about trusting me with a car since Dorothy's demise. It wasn't a good time to suggest he get over her. But even Father Timothy thought Jack should be happy his dad and Dorothy were together again.

Jack gasped. "You wrecked your car."

"Nothing like that. I'm giving her a rest. I just need a loaner."

"You lost her. You lost the Silver Bullet."

"I didn't lose her, Jack."

"I don't believe you. I want a picture. Evidence of life."

"I'll text one."

"With today's *Times* headline."

"Jeez, Jack. Can you give me a car or not?"

"I might give you Marion. If you're gentle with her. She's a lady."

Seriously?

I squinched my eyes closed and smacked my forehead for not calling Hertz.

"Thanks, Jack. Nothing bad will happen to Marion. I promise."

"I remember that's what you said about Dorothy."

"Do you remember what Father Timothy said?"

He sniffed. "It was a nice service."

"Thanks, Jack. I'll catch a ride to your shop."

"Don't think about showing up here without your mama's cannoli. I got a big crew."

"And I got a big Tupperware-full."

"My favorite is toasted almond."

"Well, today it's chocolate."

I rinsed off the bubbles, blow-dried and fastened my hair in a soft French braid. I reached for my phone a half dozen times to call Rocco. I needed to tell him I found Sam I Am. But each time I tucked it away again without pushing *Send*.

I didn't know what my brother would do if he knew Sammy was being held at the Dreamscape Motel. I wasn't entirely sure he wouldn't charge to room seven with guns drawn and sirens blazing. Sort of like Grumpy, the unlikely seer, predicted last night. But I trusted Captain Bob's solution even less. He wanted Uncle Joey to send an assassin. In the end I did what I wanted. I gave myself a day to keep my secret and stir up some trouble of my own.

I was working my way through a bowl of Cheerios and a cup of java when my cell phone boomed, "They're Coming to Take Me Away, Ha Haaa!"

I picked up. "Sophia! I was about to call you. We need to talk."

"Open your door. I'm on your porch."

Click.

I hurried down the hallway to let her in but she jammed her thumb on the bell until I got there. When I opened the door, she barreled inside.

"What's up?" I said.

"I'm a detective, dammit. I want my badge."

"You're still in training."

"I graduated."

"In one day?"

"I'm a fast learner." She stomped to the living room and plopped on the couch. "The training was intensive. Brutal. I still can't feel my legs."

"Max said you quit early."

"I quit while I could still walk. I want a badge like Cleo's."

"Talk to Cleo. I'm not sure where she got it."

That was true enough. I've always suspected she found it in a box of cereal.

"Cleo's badge looks cool. It can scare people."

"Maybe if you're eight and playing cops and robbers."

"And you have to call Max. Tell him I'm done training. Tell him I have a badge and a gun."

"A *gun?*"

"Well, I'm getting a gun."

"You tell him."

She shuddered. "I can't. The guy is brutal."

"So, you're over your crush then."

She giggled. "Are you kidding? That man can wear the shit outta a pair of jeans."

"Crap," I said.

I brought Sophie into the kitchen and made her a cup of coffee. She pulled Mama's Tupperware out of the fridge and I took it from her hands. I sprinkled some toasted almonds on top and shoved the Tupperware back in the fridge. I handed Sophie a peach.

"Sorry, Sis. The cannoli goes to Jack. I need you to drop me at the shop on your way to Holy Shih Tzu."

"I'm not changing my religion."

"God, no. What would Father Timothy do without your daily updates? Holy Shih Tzu is a lapdog rescue and adoption in Champaign."

"No one goes to Champaign."

"No one goes to Cleveland. Champaign is cool. And it's not that far."

"It's still a schlepp. Why would I go there?"

"Because you're on a case."

"I'll need a gun."

"Seriously? Yesterday you wouldn't shoot anyone."

"Yesterday I wasn't a detective."

Geesh.

I stuffed a manila envelope in her hand. "Here's the address and the adoption papers. I spoke with the foster family this morning. They're expecting you."

"Oh."

Sophie looked disappointed. I reminded myself that she was having an adventure.

I lowered my voice. "The dog you're picking up is part of a top secret operation. What you're doing today could divert a crisis for the Chicago Police Department and Bridgeport's Ninth Precinct."

Cleo's face brightened considerably.

"Make sure you're not followed. And until this case is over, Operation Thor is top secret. Don't tell anyone you left town or that you brought a dog to this house."

"Is it okay if I tell Mama? I'll need her to stay longer with the kids."

"God, no. Especially not Mama."

"I've never lied to Mama."

"What kind of daughter are you?"

I was beginning to think Sophie deserved all Mama's silver. She gnawed on her lip. "I suppose I can say I'm working late."

"Perfect. And you're still not lying."

We went to my office and I rummaged through Cleo's corner desk. There were M&M's, romance novels, two pistols, some loose ammo, and a few back issues of *PI Magazine*. I found Cleo's silver star under a Beretta Firearms catalogue. Its prickly point was dangerously close to a pack of bubble gum-flavored condoms.

"Aha! Cleo's badge. You're in luck, Sister." I slapped the silver star in her hand. "Congratulations, Detective. This is already the longest week in my life."

"You mean—?"

"Yes. The badge is yours."

I hadn't seen Sophie so excited since she was sixteen and won the Miss Bridgeport competition. She got to sit on Santa's lap during the whole Christmas parade. He looked way too cheery.

"What about Cleo? I mean when…"

Her brow furrowed and her words hung in the air.

"You mean what happens when she can't find her silver star?"

Sophie's troubled eyes blinked and she nodded.

"It's all good," I said. "I'll tell her to eat more cereal."

I left Sophie in the office and got ready to be dropped off at Jack's. I put the dishes in the sink and grabbed the Tupperware of Mama's cannoli from the fridge. I texted Chance and asked him to call me when the DNA results came in for the honey-colored hair I pulled from the intruder's head during our scuffle at Captain Bob's.

I called to Sophie from my room. "Sis, I'm ready!"

She hollered back. "How do these things fit in here?"

Before I could ask what she meant, my phone blasted "Wild One." It was my assistant, Cleo Jones. She was out of town for her sister's wedding.

I picked up. "Hey, girlfriend."

The voice on the other end was snarky. "What's going on, Cat?"

"Cleo?"

"So you do remember me."

"Do I? You've been gone three whole days."

"So, what? I'm dead to you now? Is that why you gave my job away?"

"What are you talking about?"

"Sophie. She's at my desk as we speak."

"Oh. She's helping me out when you're gone."

"What does she do there?"

"She makes me as crazy as you do."

"I doubt that's possible."

"You underestimate my sister. How'd you know she was here? Cuz if you have a camera on your desk, it's gonna be weird."

"Sophie called me. She wanted to know how to load a bullet into a chamber...."

Holy crap!

I dropped the phone and sprinted down the hall from my bedroom. There was a loud pop as I charged through the office door. The shot grazed my hair and I felt the hot breath of the bullet on my ear.

"That's how it works!" Sophie said.

I staggered back a few steps and I couldn't breathe. I grabbed the doorframe to keep from crashing.

"Oops," Sophie said. "My bad."

When I found my legs again, I crossed the room in long strides. I took a plastic storage container from the shelf behind my desk and tossed everything inside that could get Sophie in trouble. Guns, ammo, Cleo's spy toys—like the pen with a secret blade, and especially the bubble gum-flavored condoms. I left her the candy, the romance novels, and Cleo's silver star. On second thought, I took a Cadbury bar with me.

I don't know about Rocco, but when my life flashes before my eyes, I need chocolate.

"Stay," I said.

I carried Cleo's stuff to the kitchen and opened the secret compartment behind the pantry. I placed the storage container by the dusty bottles left over from Prohibition. Then I shut myself in the pantry with my back against the wall and ate my Cadbury bar. I took my time. When I returned to the office, the wobbles were gone.

"You have chocolate on your mouth," Sophie sang. She was wearing the silver star.

"No, I don't." I wiped my mouth with the back of my hand.

Sophie stared at my lips and flicked a finger at the side of her mouth. "You missed...."

I held up my hand. "Stop. No more guns until Max takes you to the shooting range."

Her lips formed a pout. "Why don't you take me?"

"Cuz I just might shoot you."

Chapter Sixteen

I dug deep in my box of smokescreens and tricks. When I stretched out on the lumpy motel mattress, I was a blue-eyed blonde. I fed the Magic Fingers massage machine a roll of quarters and read a few more chapters of my mystery while Sammy's lost brown eyes watched me from my laptop.

Yesterday's *Law and Order* marathon had played out and a flurry of *Cops* reruns played in room seven.

Bad boys, bad boys, What-cha gonna do....

I wanted to bang my head on the bedpost each time a new episode started. Baltimore cops were tackling a bad boy in an alley when someone knuckle-rapped my door.

"Housekeeping."

"One moment!" I called back.

I muted the audio, closed the laptop, and threw some towels on the bathroom floor. Then I tossed back the bedspread and rumpled the sheets before letting her in.

The housekeeper was early twenties with short brown hair and red-framed glasses. Her nametag read *Ami* and her arms were laden with linens and cleaners.

She sprayed Pine-Sol in the clean bathroom and changed the towels. She flounced across the room and swept everything that didn't move with a feather duster. Ami chewed Juicy Fruit gum with an unsettling zeal and when she'd sucked out the flavor, she spat the chewed wad in the garbage and popped two new pieces in her mouth. She offered the package to me and I helped myself to a piece and chewed.

I hate Juicy Fruit.

"How's your day going?" I said.

"In five minutes, fabulous. Your room is my last."

"If I help, you'll make it in three."

I took one side of the bed and she took the other. We stripped and changed the bedding. The mattress vibrated as we worked.

"Housekeeping work is a killer on the back," she said. "Someday I'm gonna rent a room and feed it quarters all night."

I dropped a few more quarters in the slot. "Go ahead. Give it a spin."

"I couldn't."

"I insist."

She plopped on the bed and sighed. "If I could take this home with me, I'd dump my boyfriend."

"My boyfriend and I split last month," I said. "But there was more magic in his fingers than this lumpy mattress."

"You find a new beau?"

"I dunno. I was checking out the guy in seven."

"Mr. Smith."

"I bet you get a lot of Smiths here."

She giggled. "He looks good for an older guy."

"I've been reluctant to approach him. I mean, I've made mistakes with men before."

"Who hasn't? Men make us stupid."

"What's Mr. Smith like?"

"He don't talk much. Except to his dog." She giggled. "But then…"

"Tell me."

"I dunno. I wouldn't want to date him."

"Why not?"

"He calls his dog "lady." When they walk, he dresses her in a silly pink coat. Like a girl."

"Is that a problem?"

"The dog has a penis. He hits every tree and fire hydrant he passes."

I laughed. "That's a problem."

"I wouldn't want to date a guy who can't tell the difference. Just sayin'."

"Gotcha."

"Mr. Smith is nice, though. Sort of laid back. Only saw him pissed off once. And whoa! He's got a mouth on him."

"When was that?"

"This morning. A guy called the office and left a message. Said he couldn't get ahold of him on his cell phone. I gave Mr. Smith the message."

"What was the message?"

She lowered her voice. "This is your bleeping boss. Answer your bleep bleep cell phone. Stan's bleeping appendix burst. He can't cover your bleeping shift. I need you tonight."

"I think I can fill in the blanks."

"I wouldn't answer my phone either. When you've got a week off at a sweet motel, the last thing you want is a call from the boss."

"Is that what the boss called him? Mr. Smith?"

She thought a moment and shook her head. "Russell. He said 'Russell in seven.'"

"Thanks, Ami." I pressed a fat tip in her hand. I've found when people are well compensated, they tend to keep their mouths shut.

Ami gathered her supplies and dirty linen and I opened the door. She stepped outside and gave a low whistle.

I poked my blond head around her and groaned.

Max.

The ex-spy was stalking me in Ray-Ban shades and a leather bomber jacket and a shit-ass grin. He removed the shades and his lips curled in amusement. The housekeeper wet her lips.

"Girlfriend, if that hunk of gorgeousness is your ex, take him back."

I exaggerated an eye roll and pushed past her. She scooted behind me.

"Is it true blondes have more fun?" he said.

"You're sitting on my car. Again."

Max eyes were sparking mischief. "Are you ready to come home, Love?"

Ami slugged an elbow in my ribs. "Say yes!"

"The kids and I miss you."

Ami frowned. "Kids?"

"We have dogs."

"I don't care if he's about talking orangutans. Get your ass home, girl. If you think about Mr. Smith again, slap yourself silly."

"You said Mr. Smith was cute."

"I lied."

Inga jumped on Max's legs, tail wagging. Max slid his fine bum from the hood and scratched her ears.

Ami gawked at his rippling muscles. I was pretty sure her eyes were stuck. One look at Max had thrown her in hormonal overdrive. I pushed her toward her cart and she reluctantly wheeled away. Then I stomped to the Silver Bullet and faced Max with a growl.

Max stared into my colored contacts and a small smile curved one corner of his mouth. "Don't I make your green eyes blue?"

"You're stalking me with Tino's tracker. I have a phone."

"We're supposed to be partners and you're holding out on me. You're investigating the hit-and-run."

"You don't know that. I'm at a sleazy motel. I could be stalking a cheater."

"But you're not."

I gulped a guilty sigh. "Okay, you're right."

"Who's in seven?"

"Damn, you're good."

The gold flecks danced in his brown eyes. "You've no idea," he said and my cheeks burned. He laughed.

"Your eyes shot to seven when your head popped out your door."

"Ouch." An amateur mistake.

"And there's the bogus roll of Life Savers on your dash. A tiny camera is pointed at seven's door."

"Only a spy would know that."

"Or a tech nerd, cop, or mystery buff."

The door to seven shot open and the man with a frizzy, sandy ponytail emerged with Sam I Am in tow. He wore black jeans and a Grateful Dead tee and he smelled like Brute and minty mouthwash.

Inga wasn't fooled by her friend's hot pink disguise. She tossed back her head with a joyful howl and bolted to Sam's side. Sammy whimpered and they sniffed bums; a ritual that would, in the human world, almost certainly get somebody arrested.

I blurted an awkward laugh. "My beagle has no boundaries. It's embarrassing."

Perhaps the sound of my voice clicked a memory in Sam. He made a soft cry and lunged to me. My throat hurt. I dropped to my knees and hugged him hard.

Mr. Smith's face was guarded. "Daisy don't take to people like that."

I didn't know what to say.

I giggled, acting all ditzy and blond. "Gosh. Dogs love me."

Max pulled me to my feet. "My wife's a dog whisperer. You'd hate to walk with her in a dog park."

I gave Max a playful slap.

A smile tugged at Mr. Smith's mouth. "You're right there." He took a gulp of the soda in his hand. "Say good-bye, Daisy." And he dragged Sam away.

He tossed the soda can in a bin by the office and they ambled down the street together.

"That dog knows you," Max said.

"Yep."

Sam looked back once more and lifted his leg on the first fire hydrant he found.

Max smiled. "Daisy has a surprise under that pink coat."

I made a face. "Yeah. That's Sam."

"Tell me that gender-confused dog isn't your client."

"I can't do that."

Max grinned. "Jeez, Cat. How's he paying you? In dog biscuits?"

"Sam lives with Captain Bob and Peggy. He was kidnapped from Bob's backyard."

A tic worked in his cheek. "You should've told me."

I rolled my eyes. "I know. You can kill him with your bare hands."

"That option is on the table."

"Here's the thing. Smith's not working alone. There are at least two others involved. This isn't over until we take them all down."

"What do these clowns want?"

"They're convinced Bob and Papa stole a golden lion medallion, with emerald eyes and a canary diamond mane, as Daniel lay dying in the street."

"Bullshit."

"Totally. I'm not worried about Sam at this point. Smith likes him. Last night he let him sleep on the bed with him."

"He's not a nice guy, Cat. Those are prison tattoos on his arm. He didn't do time for parking tickets."

"Agreed. But a trip to the big house doesn't make him a psycho. He could be an entrepreneur who grew wacky weed in his bathtub."

"Why are you defending this douche-canoe?"

"I'm not."

"Good. Cuz I'm going to make him pay when we get Sam."

Max reached into his pocket for a handkerchief, walked over to the recycle bin, and retrieved Mr. Smith's empty Sprite can.

"We'll have Rocco run these prints. And your client can buy us lunch."

"I hope you like dog biscuits."

Max grinned. "Breakfast of champions."

Chapter Seventeen

Rocco and Jackson were across town when I called, but they beat us to Vito and Nick's Pizzeria on West Fulton Market. When you offer my brother free food, he hits the siren.

Max and I joined them at a quiet table in the back. I kissed my brother's cheek, and plopped the bagged soda can on the table.

"What's this?" Rocco eyed the bag.

"Fingerprints of the guy who has the captain's dog."

He looked appropriately impressed. "You found Sam I Am?"

"Crazy, huh? You wouldn't think a crook would have his pizza delivered."

Rocco's face darkened. He wasn't wowed anymore. "Christ, Cat. Tell me you didn't go to this asshole's house alone."

"Uh…"

"Dammit. You should've called me."

"It wasn't his house. Mr. Smith is at a cheesy motel. I didn't want to wake you."

"Wake me, please. Was Max with you?"

"Uh, sure."

Max shot me a look and I kicked him.

"Thanks, man," Rocco said. "I owe you."

"Can you make a speeding ticket go away?"

Rocco smiled. "I got the magic touch."

Max reached in a pocket and Rocco scooped the paper from his hand.

"He'll give it to Uncle Joey," I said.

"Thanks," Max said.

Jackson growled. "Where's this sleazy motel? I say we bring Sammy home tonight."

"Damn straight," Rocco said.

"Count me in," Max said. "I'm gonna hang this asshole by his ponytail."

"Stuff a cork in the testosterone, boys," I said. "The hanging party will have to wait. Ponytail isn't the only player here. We need to ID his partners."

"Bullshit," Jackson said. "We're sending a message."

"Not today. I have a plan." I whipped out my phone and passed two pictures around.

Rocco stared at the pics. "It's Sam. What's your point?"

"The dog on the left is Sam. The other is Thor, Sam's double. Sophie's picking him up from a shelter as we speak."

Max blinked. "Your plan is to switch dogs? It's…"

"Brilliant, huh?"

"It's insane."

"With a little luck, it'll buy us time to find Smith's partners. And with Sam safe, the kidnappers lose their leverage over Bob."

Jackson growled. "Or we could skip the theatrics and make Ponytail tell us where the other clowns are."

"What if Ponytail doesn't talk?" I said. "Only a fool thinks there's no honor among thieves."

"He'll talk," Jackson said. "I'll make him."

"Tough guy," I said. "Here's the thing. The captain wants this to go away quietly. That means we can't arrest him. And you can't waterboard him."

"She's right. They hold all the cards," Rocco said. "I hate to say it, but we might need to negotiate with these sons of bitches."

Jackson scoffed. "Pay them off? No way."

"This is for the captain. That means we do this his way. You okay with that?"

"Hey," Jackson said, "I just want lunch. And some sweet vacation when I place Sam in the captain's grateful arms."

Rocco's phone buzzed. He dragged the cell from a pocket and checked the number. "It's Cam Stewart. He might be able to tell us something about this clown train." He pushed his chair back and took the call outside.

"Who's Cam Stewart?" Max said.

"Cam Stewart was the detective assigned to the Baumgarten Jewelry heist," I said. "It was never solved. But anything he has could help."

We ordered sausage pizzas and salads around. Beer for Max and me. Sodas for the cops on duty.

"You should have dessert," Max said. "This is on Cat's expense account."

"I could go for the peach cobbler," Jackson said.

Max grinned. "Make that four cobblers. A la mode. Cat's client is loaded."

Rocco returned to the table with a thumbs-up. "Cam agreed to meet us. Jackson and I will head to his house after lunch."

"Do you mind if we tag along?" I said.

"Why not?" My brother raised his glass. "I never bite the hand that feeds me."

Max tapped Rocco's Coke with his beer. "Or paw, as it were."

"Shut up," I said.

◇◇◇

Retired Detective Cam Stewart had bright hazel eyes, a stocky build, and a pool table in his living room. He lived in a man cave. The chairs hugged a wet bar, and a sixty-inch screen broadcasting ESPN swallowed a wall. The space was a frat house wet dream. I wouldn't have blinked if the guy was wearing a toga.

Jackson's eyes went glassy. "Sweet digs."

I made a wild guess. "You're not married, are you?"

Cam met my gaze levelly. "My wife's gone. Her ashes are on the mantle."

My eyes flew to a gold urn with a smattering of dazzling jewels. I winced. "I'm sorry for your loss."

Cam followed my gaze. "The gold urn is Jack, my English

"You'll love this timepiece," he said. "I have two. One in the living room. And a smaller one on my bedroom dresser."

The woman's eyes widened with interest. "Two?"

"Thank you, Mr. Baumgarten," her husband said firmly as he took her arm and hastened her outside.

The three of us were alone.

The jeweler frowned. "You."

"Max, this is my friend, Rob."

"We are in no way friends," Rob said. "My clients don't like cops snooping around. It's not good for business."

"Well it's a darn good thing we're not cops." I gave him my best smile. "I, uh, well actually, I am looking for a gift."

His cool eyes thawed. "Excellent. For whom?"

I thought fast. "It's for my assistant, Cleo Jones. She is out of town for a family wedding. I'm thinking of a small welcome home thing."

"May I suggest this delicate teardrop diamond necklace?"

"Delicate is not Cleo's look."

"She might like these classic silver hoop earrings with diamond accents."

"You're getting warmer."

"Tell me about your assistant."

"Bling. Flash. Showy baubles."

A smile tugged the corners of his mouth. "I have some bolder pieces in the back. They don't resonate with what we display in the cases."

Rob led the way to the back room. The walls were covered with pictures telling the tale of a happy childhood. Rob with grass-stained knees in his soccer uniform. Rob at the local ice cream parlor with a triple scoop. Rob riding dirt bikes with three of his friends.

We followed him to a work table with three small trays of jewelry. "These pieces are sold in our Wheaton store and on our website. Sometimes on eBay. Each piece is an original design and one of a kind."

"They're breathtaking," I said.

Max held an emerald necklace to the light and nodded appreciatively. "Tino remembers your dad was a gifted artist. You inherited his gift."

I fingered the blue sapphire drop earrings. "They're perfect. They scream Cleo. How much?"

He turned over a small tag and exposed an outrageous number. I gulped.

"That's a lot of bauble."

He smiled. "You're getting a lot of bling."

I took a measured breath. "Wrap it up. This year Santa's coming early."

"Excellent."

We returned to the front of the shop. I selected a card and wrote a note. *Welcome home. Happy Birthday. Merry Christmas. With love from Inga and Cat, your sisters in crime.*

I added a dent to my plastic. Rob popped the earrings in a black velvet box and tweaked it with a satin bow. We thanked him and walked outside. The sky was a deep blue and the sun felt good on my face. We crossed the street to the bakery and bought coffee and apple spice donuts.

"I thought you'd have some questions for Rob," I said.

"I didn't have to. Rob tipped his hand when he took us in the back."

"What did I miss?"

Max took a big bite of his donut. "Rob fences stolen jewelry."

"No!"

I wiped a trace of cinnamon sugar from his mustache.

"Yes." Max grinned. "Did you see the small, cloth bag in his desk drawer? It was quite full. I caught a glimpse of gold, maybe a watch, and what could be a diamond tennis bracelet. Rob caught me looking and closed the drawer. His face colored. Classic sign of guilt."

"Or embarrassment. Maybe he buys estate jewelry and resets the gems. Cheesy and unethical, yes. But hardly criminal."

"Jewelry that comes with a sales receipt isn't dumped together in a string-tie bag. I think Rob buys stolen high-end pieces and

"A procrastinator. I suppose she's late for work."

She had me there.

"Sophie, you have children. You bake your own bread."

"I can give you part time. Special assignments. Don't pressure me for overtime. My babies come first."

"God, yes. I can hear them crying now."

"I just talked to Mama. They've had snacks and are settling down for a nap. I can go with you to the shooting range."

"Shouldn't you be at home, getting pregnant?"

She gave a giddy laugh and I knelt beside Thor. He was thinner than Sam and a touch taller. But the coat would fill him out and the similarity between them was uncanny. A switch wouldn't fool the captain. But I was confident we could pull this off with Ponytail and his gang of thieves.

I ruffed Thor's ears. "I'll fix you a big bowl of dog food dripping in bacon fat. It might fill you out a bit. I know what bacon does to my thighs."

Sophie rubbed her Barbie thighs. She hasn't eaten bacon since George W was President.

"Shut up," I said.

I removed Thor's leash and he raced Inga around the yard. They wrestled with Inga's toys and dug up my flower bulbs.

Sophie threw a few distracting balls and buried the flower bulbs. It was a losing battle. I disappeared and returned with two tart, icy lemonades. Sophie took a sip and frowned.

"Where's the rum?"

I trotted back to the kitchen, as a sculpted babe-magnet dragged his head out of the fridge.

I swallowed a scream. "Don't do that," I said. "You scared the crap out of me."

Max grinned and took a bite of cannoli. "I talked to one of the witnesses. An RN. She was coming out of the bakery when Danny was hit. She was the first to reach his side. She said there wasn't much she could do."

"Did she see the accident?"

"Not really. She said she was totally focused on the victim and trying to figure out how she could save him. It happened a long time ago but she never forgot how powerless she felt."

"Did you ask her about the medallion?"

"She didn't see it. She said she would have remembered it if it was there."

"And you believed her."

"Totally."

I spiked the lemonades and poured two fat fingers of Uncle Joey's hijacked whiskey for Max. He sipped the liquid amber and smiled.

"I don't know who that second lemonade's for. But I can see you love me more."

I smiled. "Your glass has more courage. You might need it."

"I'm a fearless guy, Babe."

Sophia tromped in the kitchen. "Where's my…?"

Her voice faltered. She saw the delicious piece of man meat, and her cheeks pinked.

"Max," she breathed.

"Max is here to take you to the shooting range," I said.

He tossed the contents of his glass down his throat.

"Wee!" Sophie squealed and threw her arms around him.

Max's eyes flashed terror. He wriggled back but she was on him like white on rice.

Help! Max mouthed.

I blew him a kiss. "Fearless, Babe."

◇◇◇

The dogs licked their bowls clean and fell asleep by the fire. It was time to bring in reinforcements. I called my computer genius friend. My cousin's fiancé is three hundred pounds of loveable.

Roger dispensed with the hellos. "Where's Sam I Am?" he demanded. "Have you saved him yet?"

"Soon. I need a little help from my favorite geek."

"Is it dangerous?"

"Not if we're lucky."

"I have a rabbit's foot."

"So we're good?"

"Definitely. You introduced me to Ginny. I owe you."

I laughed. "I'm here to collect. I found a dog that looks like Sam. We need to switch them."

"You don't think Bob will notice?"

"Not Bob. The kidnappers."

"Okay. So you want me to help you grab Sam and leave a sacrificial lamb in his place."

"That would be Thor."

"It's an inspired plan. Not for Thor, of course."

"Thor will be fine. I promise I'll get him out."

"I'll be there when you do."

"Deal."

Roger was quiet a moment. "You're sure there's no other way?"

"Do you have a better idea?"

"I was thinking about your crazy Cousin Frankie. He would happily put a couple rounds in these guys."

"Plan B, Roger. Plan B."

◇◇◇

I dropped Thor off with Roger and told Inga she could have a sleepover at Mama's. My night was looking uncertain at best. But Mama would feed her an outrageous number of sausages. Papa would give her his last bite of cream cake and she'd lick his dish clean. She'd sleep between them tonight and they would rub her tummy and sing the lullaby Nonna sang to me when I was a child. Grandparents are a hard act to follow.

Mama was on the phone when I let myself in the back door. Mama was baking for the annual school fundraiser and the heady essence of cinnamon filled my senses. Her pastries are the hit of the auction. One year her lasagna bolognese bought much needed new playground equipment.

I leaned over the *sfogliatella*, the rich creamy custard escaping the flaky layers of pastry. Mama reached over and slapped my hand with a wooden spoon. There would be no freebies today. If I wanted one, I'd have to go to the auction like everyone else.

"It's not like Bob to not call," Mama said. "I haven't seen him, and Tony hasn't said anything. I'll have Tony check on Bob when he gets home."

Mama was talking to Peggy. The captain's wife was worried about him. Bob was avoiding her calls and I couldn't blame him. Peggy was like Mama on steroids. She's one of the most intuitive people I know. Bob was in big trouble here. And Peggy would know it in a red-hot minute.

Mama's eyes shot to me and I gulped. "Caterina, have you seen Captain Bob?"

I shook my head fiercely. "No, I haven't."

"My daughter has seen Bob," Mama said and slapped the phone in my hand. "And you should go to confession for lying to your mama."

Crap. "Hello, Mrs. Maxfield," I said. "Are you enjoying your time with your sister?"

"Thanks for asking, Cat. She's home from surgery and recovering nicely. She's glad her uterus is gone. It kept falling out and she had to keep pushing it back up. Can you imagine?"

I was trying not to.

"Give her our love," I said.

"I will." Peggy's voice was troubled. "I'm worried about Bob, Cat. Something's going on and he won't talk to me more than a few minutes. He says everything's fine."

"I dunno," I said.

"Spill it," Peggy said. "Your mama says you saw him."

"Tell her," Mama said.

"Yesterday. He said he was fine. I ran into him when I was shopping."

"He was lying," Peggy said. "Where was that?"

"He was parked on the street by the bakery."

"Which one?"

"Across from Baumgarten's Jewelry."

Her sharp, intake of breath sounded like a groan. "Oh, God."

For a moment I thought we were disconnected. "Mrs. Maxfield?"

"I'm coming home. As soon as I make arrangements for my sister's daughter to stay with her. Let me speak to your mama."

I handed off the phone, stunned. How did this happen? What did I say? The captain told me to keep my big mouth shut. He was gonna be pissed.

And if Peggy is upset now, just wait 'til she learns Sammy is missing.

That's when I knew Bob told his wife what happened the day Daniel was struck down in the street. And Papa had not. Cuz when I mentioned Baumgarten's Jewelry, there was anguish in Mrs. Maxfield's voice. Mama, however, didn't bat an eye. She rolled out another batch of *sfogliatella*.

Bob and Papa were the good guys. No matter how I wracked my brain, I couldn't imagine what they'd done. And now, for the first time, I wasn't sure I wanted to know.

The women spoke briefly and Mama hung up. She took one look at my guilty face and rapped my hand again with the wooden spoon.

"Ouch!"

"What did you say, Caterina? Now Peggy is upset. She says she's coming home."

"I'm a dead woman, Mama. The captain is going to kill me."

I robo-walked to the back door and Mama called me back. I turned around. Inga, her brown eyes sorrowful, was pressed against her Nonna's legs. My partner knew I was done for. And she abhors violence

Mama pressed a warm *sfogliatella* in my hand. She knew I was a goner too.

◇◇◇

The James Bond theme song blared from my phone as I fired up the engine.

"Hey, spy man," I said.

"Gattina!" Tino's voice answered.

Gattina is a term of endearment that literally means, *little cat*. It's Tino's nickname for me and it always makes me smile. It also makes me think he doesn't know I tower over him.

"I can't find Max," he said. "He doesn't answer his cell."

"Max can't hear his phone. He took Sophie to the shooting range."

"Sophia with a gun?"

"Scary, huh?"

Tino chuckled. "I'd say your little sister is a DeLuca after all. Not switched at birth as you suspected."

"Bite your tongue."

"How is the investigation coming?"

"We're in the beginning stages. We'll get there."

"I want the man who killed my friend. When you have a name, give it to me. And then forget about it."

"You're bossy."

"And yet, you adore me."

I laughed. "Do you want me to find Max for you?"

"It can wait. I have an address for Felix."

"The guy who did odd jobs."

"Felix had physical challenges; unsteady when he walked. He was born with a crooked spine, I think. He was a good worker. Danny was nuts about the kid. He enjoyed having him around."

"I remember he was outside washing windows when Danny was hit. It had to be tough on him."

"We can't imagine. I hate to dredge up the memories for him again. But he might know something about the driver."

"I can give Max the message when I see him. They should be back soon."

He rattled off the address and I scratched it on the back of an old receipt.

"How'd you find him?" I said.

"A guy in Social Security owed me a favor. I asked him to search Medicare disability recipients. He said the address is in an assisted living facility. Upscale with private apartments and a shared recreational center and dining room. Even a gym. He said you gotta have some serious cash to live there."

"Rich parents?"

"Felix was abandoned on the steps of St. Michael's when he was a baby. He didn't have a pot to piss in when Danny was around."

"Maybe he won the lottery."

"Be sure to ask him. I want you to go with Max. Felix is a timid guy. And Max can appear big and fierce."

"I'm fierce."

Tino barked a belly laugh. "If you're lucky, Felix will play the piano for you. Ask him anything. If he doesn't know it, hum the tune and he'll play it. He's a freaking genius. Considering, that is…"

"What?"

"You'll see. You'll go, won't you?"

I smiled. "I wouldn't miss it."

I tossed the phone in my bag and punched the address in my GPS. I kicked the engine in gear and I was off to see the man with the crooked spine.

Chapter Nineteen

The assisted living facility felt like an upscale retirement complex. Except the residents were younger and I knew each had a disability. There was no answer when I knocked on Felix's door but a neighbor riding a scooter led me to a game room and pointed him out to me.

Felix was fortyish; a small, thin man with mousy brown hair, and wire-rimmed glasses. At the moment he was playing a game of chess. And he was going in for the kill. He'd captured nearly every one of his opponent's chess pieces and the guy wasn't happy. He wore a Luke Skywalker tee and the Force wasn't with him.

Skywalker's eyes widened as Felix's queen descended on his doomed King.

"Don't do it, Felix. Don't do it," he snarled.

Felix gave a wicked grin and his queen pounced on the King. They tussled and the King crashed on his back.

"Checkmate!" Felix shouted.

Skywalker leapt to his feet and his arm swept the board. The board flew to the floor and all the King's men took flight.

The other residents barely blinked.

"Larry, Larry," an employee said. "Can you go to a happy place now?"

"He goaded me!"

"It's true," Felix said. "I'm sorry, Larry."

Larry looked sheepish. "It was a good game."

"It was a slaughter," a young woman giggled. "Nobody beats Felix in chess."

"You got that right," Larry admitted.

He rescued the scattered pieces and a few friends helped. They'd done this before. With the chess set reordered, Larry moved across the room and ran explosively on the treadmill. His feet pelted the walking belt. I guessed there was a glitch in Larry's gray matter. Like bi-polar on steroids.

"Who wants to play me now?" Felix said and I shot to the table before he could tie up a new game. I thrust out my hand.

"Hi, Felix, I'm Cat DeLuca. I want to talk to you about your friend, Daniel Baumgarten."

"Mr. B is dead."

"I understand you and he were close."

His face darkened and his hand stroked something on his lap. I stretched my neck to see the stuffed animal on his legs.

"Nice bear," I said.

"Mr. B bought it for me at a game."

The bear wore a blue baseball cap with a big red C. "Did we win?"

He thought a moment. "Sammy Sosa got a walk-off grand slam in the ninth. We creamed the Cardinals, nine to five. We had hot dogs and ice cream. I had chocolate fudge, and Mr. B had pistachio."

He smiled, delighted with himself.

Felix was mentally challenged. But like many challenged individuals, he was utterly brilliant in specific areas. He played chess very well. And Tino remembered he's a master pianist.

"Can we go somewhere to talk? I'd like to ask you a few questions about the day Mr. B died."

Felix pushed back his chair and stood with some difficulty. He hunched over as he walked, gripping a wooden cane with a detailed carving of a lion's head as the handle. We took the long hall slowly, the crooked spine protesting every step he took. The silence felt awkward and I tried to fill some of it with small talk.

"Danny must have liked you very much."

Felix smiled shyly. "Mr. B took me to the bakery across the street. Every Wednesday."

"Tomorrow is Wednesday."

Felix kept walking.

"I stopped by Baumgarten's Jewelry today," I said. "Rob was there. He told me to say hi."

"Mr. B is dead."

"Yes. I'm sorry."

"I kept Mr. B's plunder safe."

"Mr. B had plunder? Like a pirate?"

Felix laughed. "Mr. B brought diamonds from South Africa. Like a pirate. And he brought me this walking stick."

"It's very cool."

He tapped his ebony stick on the floor. "Mr. B said the lion was like me. I'm a Leo."

"You must be very brave."

Felix nodded solemnly. "I would have saved Mr. B."

"I'm sure you would have."

"I didn't see the bad men coming."

"*What?*"

Felix's shuffling feet stopped and he pushed a heavy oak door with an exit sign. I stepped outside.

"Are we going to the terrace?" I said.

"You're going home now."

"Wait! I need to talk to you."

"I don't want to talk. There was too much blood."

"Tell me about the bad men."

"They give me bad dreams." He slammed the door. I tried the knob but it wouldn't open without a key card.

I shot to a window and watched the crooked man hobble down the hall.

"What bad men?" I demanded to no one at all.

◇◇◇

I made a 7-11 stop for juice and snacks. I was ready to hunker down for a long stretch.

The housekeeper said Mr. Smith had been called into work tonight. Maybe he'd blow off his job. But if he made his shift and left Sammy in the motel or car, switching dogs would be a cakewalk.

I settled in on the lumpy mattress and brought Sammy up on the computer screen. He was tied to the bedrail again, eyes big and brown and sad. I tuned in the audio. Dr. Phil was talking to parents who lost kids to gun violence. It was a gut-wrenching segment. Ponytail blew his nose hard but maybe he was coming down with a cold.

The hours dragged on. I ate all the chips and a bag of M&M's. I gave myself a mani-pedi with Road House Blues nail polish. I fed a handful of quarters to the greedy Magic Fingers and was lulled by its soft buzz and rhythmic shudder. I must have dozed because a knock on the room next door shot me straight up in bed. The computer screen went black. I fell over myself getting to the window.

I opened the door a crack and caught a flash of honey blond and green scarf disappear into room seven.

I turned up the audio. Ponytail muted the TV. "Thanks for taking Sam, Saleen. I'll drop by and pick him up on my way home from work."

"He looks sad."

"He's okay. How's your mom?"

"Not good. I see her slipping away. We don't have much time."

"He'll pay, Saleen. I promise. We'll have thirty g's in a few days and she'll begin treatments Monday."

"I hope so."

"She's strong. She'll beat this. And someday she'll dance at your wedding."

I seized my purse and dumped the contents on the bed. I grabbed the keys to the Silver Bullet and raced outside in my bunny slippers. In a moment my head was in the trunk and my hands fumbled in my box of hotshot tricks for my GPS transmitter. It was in a plastic case with two heavy duty magnets and two AA batteries. It would send a signal to my phone and allow me to track her vehicle wherever she went.

I closed the trunk and scanned the parking lot. Two cars had arrived at the motel after me. But the engine under the red MINI Cooper's hood was still hot.

I dropped my keys on the ground and knelt beside the Cooper's rear tire. I reached my hand behind the back left wheel, stretching my fingers as far as I could, and secured the magnets. Then I picked up the keys and bounced to my feet.

I scootched to my room and slid inside. The woman Ponytail called Saleen stepped outside with Sam I Am in tow. He lifted his leg on the Silver Bullet's tire as he passed.

"Little stinker," I said.

Saleen took Sammy to the MINI Cooper and lifted him in her arms. She opened her door and placed him on the seat beside her. Then she held his face between her palms and kissed his head.

"Oh, crap," I thought. "I like her."

I tugged a hoodie over my head and waited for the MINI Cooper to pull onto the street. Racing outside I fired up Jack's loaner. I was hot on her tail. Saleen blazed her way to West Pershing Street and followed it all the way to the Brighton Park neighborhood. She grabbed Sam I Am and they disappeared in a yellow house with blue trim.

I stepped outside the car and did a few stretches. It was a quiet street and if there was a nosy neighbor like mine, I didn't see her gawking from a window. I ran around the block and down the alley. The yellow house had a big, fenced backyard with an herb garden. Ivy climbed up the back wall and a spray of yellow and purple irises bordered the house. A kitchen window looked out on the alley but a large dogwood afforded some cover.

The street lights blinked on. It would be dark soon. I jogged back to the car and called Roger. It was time to bring Thor.

◇◇◇

The gate was fixed with a padlock. I climbed over the fence and hid in a dark corner of the yard behind the dogwood tree. I asked Roger to park close by on the cross street and wait for my call. He said he had a bucket of chicken and if I wanted some, I should call soon.

When the back porch light popped on, the woman Pony-tail called Saleen stepped onto the porch. "Do your business, love," she said. "And then you'll cuddle with Mom and keep her company."

Saleen closed the door and I beeped Roger.

"Sam I Am, come here, boy," I whispered.

There was a whimper and in a moment he was in my arms.

The pink coat was fastened with Velcro. One rip, a pull over the head, and Voila! Nature boy.

Roger was waiting at the fence with the sacrificial lamb. I passed Sam over and grabbed Thor. Thor didn't get the sweater thing. He was far less cooperative. We wrestled and came to an understanding. When the sweater was snug I told him he was beautiful and hugged him tight. I would be back, I promised. And then I gave him a dog biscuit from my pocket.

In the wonderful world of dogs, I was forgiven.

I put Thor on the ground and he barked wildly. I jumped the fence, hopped in the car, and Roger hit the gas hard.

"Roger," I said. "This is Sam I Am. Sam, this is Roger."

Roger smiled. "Sam I Am, I am enormously pleased to meet you."

Sammy thought Roger's breath smelled delicious. He wagged his tail and poked his nose at the bucket of gnawed chicken bones.

Chapter Twenty

I came back a few hours later. The yellow house was dark downstairs but the bedroom lights upstairs didn't go out until after midnight. I gave them an hour to reach a deep REM sleep. I made one last leap over the fence and let myself in the back door.

I swept the flashlight across the kitchen and dropped the bug into a dry daisy basket flower arrangement in the middle of the kitchen table. The bug was motion- and voice-activated. It would reach up to thirty feet in every direction but would only last a limited time on its battery.

I studied the family pics in the hallway. At first there were four. Mama and Papa and Saleen and a little brother. In the last pics of four, the boy appeared increasingly thin and pale. And then there were three. Their smiles seemed more forced after that.

I thumbed through a pile of mail on a small table. There was a letter to Saleen Nelson from Chicago State University, inquiring if she was still interested in fall enrollment. There were outrageous medical bills addressed to Rana Nelson that included some chemotherapy. And a number of brochures describing an alternative cancer immunology treatment. It's revolutionary, promising, and expensive.

Ponytail had asked how Saleen's mother was. Her answer was that she wasn't good. Rana Nelson was running out of time.

The kidnappers needed money for treatment. It was their one last hope. It's why they were coming after Bob and Papa now. They were trying to save Saleen's mama.

I get it. It's what families do. I'm not saying I'd kidnap a dog in Saleen's shoes. But if Mama or Papa or even my switched-at-birth sister were dying, I'd move heaven and hell to save them.

Upstairs a bedroom door opened and I heard Thor growl. "What is it, boy?" a woman's voice said. "There's nobody downstairs."

Thor exploded into a fury of barks and tiny feet pattered down the steps. I flew across the kitchen and out the door.

I ran to my car and turned on the receiver. After a few minutes, the bug I planted in the dry flowers started talking.

"Nobody's gonna sleep tonight with that barking dog," Saleen said.

"He'll settle in," Pops said. "We'll sleep fine."

I heard water run. "I'll make tea for Mom. Want some?"

"Please."

"Honey?"

"Hmm."

"Hey," Saleen said, "what happened to his collar?"

I stopped breathing. Crap. How could I forget Sammy's collar?

There was a long silence. "What did Marco say when you asked about tomorrow?" Saleen asked.

"He's in." I could hear water begin to bubble on the stove.

Saleen sounded angry. "It's the kid's fault."

"He's not a kid anymore."

"He's not getting away with murder. He's gonna pay. He owes us, Pops. He owes Mom."

Pops was quiet a long moment. When he spoke again, his voice was tired. "I never wanted to involve you, Pumpkin."

"You didn't. I crashed the party."

Murder? My chest felt heavy. Was it possible they were talking about the Baumgarten hit? Did it have anything to do with Papa and Captain Bob's dark secret? Was there another player involved who was the guy to go after? I only knew a den of thieves just upped the ante. Sam I Am was safe. It was time to call off the troops. We needed some answers before we confronted the kidnappers.

There was the rattle of dishes and footsteps but no more conversation. After a while I decided they'd gone to bed.

I drove back to the Dreamscape and flopped on top of the covers. I dragged my bag onto the bed and rifled through it.

"Dammit," I said and tossed the bag on the floor.

I was out of quarters.

◇◇◇

I heard the obnoxious beep beep beep of Bob's alarm clock first. And then the padding of slippered feet on the hardwood floor above me. The flushing of a toilet.

Bob was a busy guy. And he hadn't been answering my calls. I thought he might appreciate some company. And even if he didn't, who brings a gun to breakfast?

That would be Bob.

I poured two cups of Columbian roast coffee and settled back in the kitchen chair to wait for the captain. A Smith & Wesson appeared around the corner first, the arm attached to it was draped in a black satin robe. An image of a bat was stitched on the sleeve.

"Are you actually wearing a Batman robe?" I said.

The captain growled and his head poked out. "You broke into my house, Caterina. I could shoot you. It would almost be an accident."

"You're much too afraid of Mama for that."

He reluctantly lowered his arm. The black satin robe with a giant yellow-and-black bat across his chest stepped into the room. A hood with bat ears hung off his back, and big yellow letters, announced I AM BATMAN.

"Do something about your security system, Bob. At least make it a challenge."

"You need help, Caterina. See a doctor, for God's sake."

"You gave me no choice. You won't take my calls. You instructed your desk sergeant to throw me out. I'm bustin' my butt to help you. Why didn't you tell me the kidnappers contacted you?"

"They didn't."

"Liar, liar. Forty g's. Ring a bell?"

Bob growled and took a few sips of coffee and blew a sigh. "Okay. So they want forty thousand dollars. I don't have it. Even if I did, I wouldn't give it to them. I didn't steal a goddamn necklace."

"It was a gold medallion. The lion had emerald eyes. Shimmery diamonds in the mane."

"Stop staring at my robe."

"I can't help myself. That's a really special robe."

"It was a Christmas gift from the grandkids."

"Don't make it weird."

"Peggy makes me wear it."

"She's not here. Unless she got here sooner than…"

I stopped myself.

The beady black eyes balked.

"Oops," I said.

"Oh, God. You talked to Peggy."

I opened the white bakery bag. "Have a lemon crème."

He sank on the chair. "You opened your big mouth and Peggy's on her way home."

I heaved a sigh. "I'm sorry, Bob. I wanted to tell you the good news first."

His eyes darkened on the revolver on the table. "Leave the donuts on the table and run. Before I reach that piece, so help me…"

For one unsettling moment I thought he meant it. "I have Sam I Am," I blurted. "He's safe. I rescued him last night."

The murderous expression in his dark eyes morphed to astonished joy. He looked happy enough to kiss me. I found that face even more disturbing.

"Sam is safe? Why isn't he here?"

"Because the kidnappers believe they still have him. For just another day or two, I need you to play along."

"I won't do it."

"You will."

And I told Bob why.

◇◇◇

I pulled Jack's loaner into the motel lot and parked behind the

Silver Bullet. My head dropped on the steering wheel and I closed my eyes. I was exhausted and I wanted to go home. I'd hardly slept in days. I hated this motel and its lumpy mattress. I missed Savino. All the quarters in the world couldn't compete with the magic in his fingers.

When I lifted my head my eyes caught a shimmering of light on the pavement by the Silver Bullet's driver's door.

"Oh no, no," I murmured. "You didn't break my window."

I tumbled outside and stomped over to the scattering of broken glass. My driver's window was smashed. The phone charger was untouched, new stereo plate and camera undisturbed in the glove box. Only the bogus roll of Life Savers, the hidden camera aimed at room seven, was gone.

"Dammit, dammit, dammit," I said. I was exhausted, and irritable and a bit PMS'y.

A soft voice spoke behind me. "Babe."

I turned around and Savino took me in his arms. His strong arms wrapping me in a cocoon of safety. I breathed deep. He smelled like my lavender shampoo.

"You slept at my house," I said.

"You didn't come home. Are you on Bob's case?"

I nodded. "I got a little shut-eye here."

"Some jackass broke your window." He glanced around. "I don't suppose there's a surveillance camera on this motel."

"Not anymore."

I pulled him against me and kissed him. "How did you know I was here?"

"I tracked your phone."

"Seriously? Doesn't anyone call anymore?"

"I called a dozen times. I was worried."

I dragged out my cell and winced. My ringer was off.

"I turned my phone off last night when I rescued Sam I Am from the kidnappers."

"You rescued Sam? Tell me you weren't alone."

"I had Roger. He's big and scary."

"He's as scary as the Pillsbury Doughboy. And he's too nice to shoot someone. I know he doesn't have a gun."

"I do."

"It's in your dresser at home. I checked."

He lifted me onto the Silver Bullet's hood and kissed me again.

I heard a familiar smack and I smelled Juicy Fruit. I looked behind Chance and the housekeeper arched her brow reproachfully. She smacked her gum again.

"Damn, girl. Look at you carrying on with this hunka man. Does Max know?"

One of Savino's brows lifted. "Max?"

Ami rocked back, hands on hips. It was a posture of moral outrage and carnal envy. "Max is her husband, dammit. Girlfriend, what is your problem? You think you have to have Mr. Smith too?"

Both of Savino's brows were on high alert. "Who's Mr. Smith?"

"Stop," I said and turned to the housekeeper. "Ami, don't you have some work to do?"

"I'll check on room seven first." She rolled her eyes. "I expect you need fresh sheets in six."

"My room is fine. The sheets are clean."

"Home with your *husband*?" She flounced to her cart for an armful of towels and washcloths and a few bars of cheap-ass soap.

She rapped on Ponytail's door. "Housekeeping!"

The sound unleashed a fury of barking. Thor might look like Sam but he was way more vocal.

"Mr. Smith?" When there was no answer she let herself in.

"Is there something you want to tell me?" Chance said.

"Ami thinks I'm shameless."

"If she was a man, I'd punch her."

"You're not curious about what she said?"

He kissed the tip of my nose. "I trust you."

"That might be the hottest thing you ever said to me." I slid off the hood and caught his hand. "Come to my room. The bed's lumpy but it's got a Magic Fingers machine."

He checked his watch and smiled. "I've got a pocketful of quarters and I'm not due in court 'til noon."

A blood-chilling scream cut the air. It was Ami.

"Wait here," Savino said.

"Not a chance." I pushed past him and dashed into seven. We raced past Thor, tied to a foot of the bed, and into the bathroom.

The room smelled of Brute and Juicy Fruit gum. The housekeeper stood at the foot of the tub. The towels had fallen to her feet and a strangled whimper came from her throat. I braced myself and looked past her. Ponytail was lying in the tub. He'd taken his last bath.

He'd been in the water long enough for his fingers and toes to wrinkle like prunes. A soggy bar of soap drifted in the water and a hairdryer floated between his legs. There was surprise in his unseeing eyes. I guessed the killer let himself in and discovered Ponytail in the bath. If he brought a gun, he didn't have to use it. The hairdryer on the sink made it too bloody easy.

I felt a crushing wave of sadness. What kind of monster would do such a thing?

Ami's voice quivered. "Is Mr. Smith d-d—"

"He's gone," Savino said gently.

"How…?"

"A hairdryer and a hundred twenty volts of electricity," I said.

"But Mr. Smith's hair isn't wet. Why…?"

Her eyes bugged and her voice pierced like nails on a chalkboard.

"Murder!??"

"Cat, if you take Ms.—"

"Ami Snow," she shrieked.

"If you would take Ms. Snow outside, I'll call this in."

The woman was in shock and her legs were like lead. I dragged her outside. Then I unchained Thor from the bed and carried him to my room. I bought a bottle of water from the vending machine.

"Drink this." I put the bottle in Ami's hand and it fell to the floor.

"Yesterday you were blond."

"Not today."

"You're a bit of a bosh, you know. No offense. Just sayin'."

I picked up the bottle of water and waited for her to drink some.

"Who would do such a thing to Mr. Smith?" she wailed.

"The cops will figure it out. I'm not sure it helps but there'll be justice for Mr. Smith."

I wasn't holding my breath. Only twenty-eight percent of last year's murders were solved.

Ami's voice was a hoarse whisper. "Was it Max?"

"What?"

"The way you were throwing yourself at Mr. Smith…"

"It wasn't Max."

"I wouldn't blame him." She didn't believe me. "People kill for two reasons. Love and money."

"So now you're an expert."

"Here are the facts. Max loves you. And Mr. Smith didn't have money. If he did, he wouldn't be in this dump."

"So?"

"So obviously Max whacked Mr. Smith. It was a crime of passion."

"That makes no sense."

"It's a gift. I got a sixth sense."

"You got a screw loose."

"I see things. I could be a detective like Erin Lindsay on *Chicago PD.*" She air-tapped her eyes. "Nobody pulls the wool over these baby blues."

Chapter Twenty-one

I called my mechanic. "Jack, this is Cat."

He blew a long-suffering sigh. "What have you done to Marion?"

"Who's Marion?"

"The car I loaned you. Against my better judgment."

Jack has an odd relationship with his cars. He names them and he coddles them. And he's furious if I blow one up.

"Marion is fine, Jack."

"No wrecks? No bullet holes? No C4?"

"She's perfect. Unfortunately, some jerk busted a window on my Honda. I'm at the Dreamscape Motel. Would you send someone over for it? I'll leave a key under the seat."

"My nephew Devin is here."

"Perfect."

"That's it? You don't want to remind me that Devin is a screw-up?"

"Ancient history. He's probably over trying to kill me. I hope he's doing well."

"Are you feeling okay? I don't want you driving Marion if you're having a seizure or something."

"I'm fine. I'll return Marion when I pick up the Silver Bullet."

"In one piece, Caterina. I want this one back in one piece."

"Jack, you know I can't make promises."

◇◇◇

The cops arrived in a fury of blue lights and screaming sirens. They came as the pudgy clerk who checked me into the motel had dreamed. And now he was pissed at me. His little fat fist pounded my door.

"Sonya Ollson! I know you're in there."

"Am not!" I rocked Thor on the bed. "Go away, Bert. No one's home."

"I knew you were trouble, missy!"

I heard Chance's voice after that and Grumpy seemed to melt away.

Savino spoke with the first responders and made a statement. Ami would tell the cops that Max murdered Ponytail in a fit of jealous rage. They would come for me but I wasn't worried. Chicago's Ninth is chockablock full of DeLuca cops and their friends. The only one out to get me is Detective Ettie Opsahl. And nobody's got her back.

The cop who came to question me was my crazy Cousin Frankie. Savino followed him in and stood, arms crossed, by the door.

Frankie looked around the room with a goofy grin. "Hard times, Caterina?"

"You're hilarious."

"Why you wanna hang around a dump like this when you got a nice place of your own?"

"That's none of your business."

"According to the housekeeper…"

"Ami Snow is delusional."

"You're not sleeping here alone. You and Max are sharing this room. And he's not the only man she's seen here."

Savino's fingers tightened but his face was flat.

"I'm working a case, dumb ass. Max is assisting me."

"Does this case involve the stiff next door?"

"I'm not at liberty to discuss my clients."

"I could arrest you for obstruction."

"Mama would whip your ass."

"What do you know about the victim?"

"Nothing, really."

"He was in the bathtub. Naked."

"He was taking a bath."

"Would you say there was something girlie about him? Was Mr. Smith a homo?"

"*What?*"

"What I'm getting is a lover's quarrel gone south. Two fags argue. The one in the tub was being a douche. His partner throws a hairdryer at him. Mr. Smith is toast."

Savino swallowed a laugh.

"You're a bonehead, Frankie." I said.

"What's that supposed to mean?"

"It means I can't believe my assistant is dating you."

A grin split his face from ear to ear. "Cleo says I'm the smartest guy she knows."

"Well, she's a bonehead too."

The door burst open and Rocco covered the room in three strides. His partner, Jackson, was close behind.

My brother sat beside me on the bed. "We heard the callout on the radio. Are you okay?"

I nodded. "I'm fine. But Ponytail didn't deserve to die like that."

Frankie scribbled *"Ponytail"* in his notebook.

"The prints came back on your soda can. Vic's name was Marcus Russell. Forty-three years old. Did a nickel in Joliet for possession of stolen property. A truckload of flat screen TVs wandered into his storage locker. He was released last month."

"He was kind to Sam," I said. "That counts for something."

"We'll get the son of a bitch, I promise."

Frankie cleared his throat and tried to look important. "The vic was hosed by a homo lover. Or maybe Max. Max is on the short list of suspects."

"Max?"

"He and Cat got something going on here. They're—"

Rocco was on his feet; his hand was on Frankie's throat. My cousin gulped for air.

"Disrespect my sister again, Francesco, and you'll be eating carpet."

Jackson smiled. "And then his mama will finish you."

Rocco released him and Frankie gasped an awkward laugh. "Can't nobody take a joke?"

Rocco tousled Thor's head. "You're safe now, Sam."

"I wanna deliver him to the captain," Jackson said. "Collect me some va-ca with pay."

"Too late," I said. "This is Thor. Sam's at home."

Rocco whistled. "You pulled it off, Sis. I didn't think you could manage the switch."

"I got mad skills, Bro."

He kissed my cheek and his partner followed him to the door. "We'll head next door and see how *C.S.I.* is doing. Jackson and I want this case."

Savino closed the door, turned, and faced Frankie. There was something behind his eyes I hadn't seen before. My cousin's bluster drained like the air out of a balloon.

"Your Cousin Rocco was too generous. I don't give second chances."

Savino landed a brutal blow to Frankie's solar plexus. Knocking him to the ground. He lay gasping for air.

Then he pulled me to my feet and kissed me. "Go home and get some rest. I'll bring dinner tonight."

We stepped over Frankie and I closed the door behind us.

◇◇◇

Ginny was home when I drove Thor to Roger's house. When she saw him she squealed and made baby goo goo sounds. She captured him in her arms and hugged him tight. Then she put him down to play with Sam I Am.

Ginny is a computer whiz. She was serious and dowdy and all left brain before she met Roger. She wasn't a squealer or a hugger and I hadn't heard her "goo" since we were two. Love looked good on her.

She was more confident and her smile was radiant. My cousin was getting all soft and marshmallowy like Roger.

Ginny brewed a pot of French roast and put out a plate of crème cakes and *sfogliatella*. I recognized Mama's signature pastries that she bakes for the school fundraiser.

"How did you wrangle these from Mama's kitchen?"

She laughed. "Roger has a conflict and will miss the auction. But he made an insane contribution to the school fund and your Mama gets the credit. She deserves it. She's agreed to provide pastries for Roger's employees once a month for a year."

"She'll love it as much as Roger. Father Timothy must think he's died and gone to heaven."

She laughed. "He plans to repave the courtyard and purchase new playground equipment with the donation."

I hugged her. "You two are amazing. How are the wedding plans coming? Should I begin organizing a bachelorette party?"

"Make it naughty. I was a late bloomer. I'll probably never see another naked man. I deserve one night of indiscretion before I get married."

"I'll hire a stripper."

"Hire a bunch. Maybe the entire Chippendale's entourage."

I laughed. "Gotcha. I'll up my game.

Ginny was going big. She was marrying a big guy with an even bigger heart and a whole lotta money. It's all good.

Ginny gave a wicked grin. "Speaking of tying the knot, I hear you could be the next to fall."

"Huh?"

"Your mama and Chance's mama have big plans for your first anniversary. A boat cruise, a party, Father Timothy on hand. A copy of the Marriage Sacrament in his pocket."

"*Et tu*, Gin?"

She laughed. "You two are great together. He's perfect for you."

"Savino snores," I said. "But, thanks for the heads-up."

I gathered Sam in my arms and her brow furrowed. "You're not taking Thor, are you?"

"No way."

She clapped her hands. That's when I knew I'd forget to ever pick him up.

At the car I checked my iPhone and pulled up the tracker app to locate Saleen's MINI Cooper. She was parked near the Dreamscape Motel and Ponytail's cold, wet body.

I zoomed to the motel where a sea of Chicago's finest was still in force. Their blue lights flashed and an officer hurried the looky-lou traffic along.

The MINI Cooper was parked across the street from the motel. I drove around the block and pulled to the curb a few cars behind her. Sammy nuzzled against me and I held him in my arms.

It felt as if a long time passed before the Medical Examiner's men carried Ponytail out on a stretcher. They wheeled his body into the back of the coroner's van. Saleen covered her face with her hands and wept.

I dropped the binoculars on the seat and started the car and jammed it in gear. I drove to Captain Bob's house and opened the door. Sammy bounded up the porch steps. I picked the lock one more time and he raced inside. I found Sammy's dishes and filled them with fresh water and food. Then I watched him eat and promised his papa would be home soon.

There was a metallic click of a key turning the lock. I held my breath.

"Sam I Am!" Peggy called. "Where are you? Mommy's home!"

Sammy made an odd sound that was something between a yelp and a sob. He would tell Peggy everything. I could only hope she wouldn't understand.

I bolted out the back door and to the street as a cab pulled away from the curb. I was hungry but too physically and emotionally exhausted to eat. I drove home and fell on my soft, warm bed and slept.

Chapter Twenty-two

I wasn't ready to get up when the sun screamed through my window. I resisted the urge to bury my head under the pillow and I kicked my feet and forced them to touch the floor. I hit the shower and dressed in jeans and a scoop-necked tee. I needed coffee.

I tromped outside as Mrs. Pickens was picking up her mail. I thought I heard her humming. I pointed the loaner my mechanic named Marion to Felix's residence. I found him in the sunroom thumbing through a big picture book on American Presidents.

Felix wasn't thrilled to see me. "Go away."

"I like reading about the Presidents too. I went to Washington D.C. once with my cousin."

"Did you see the Lincoln Memorial?"

"It's even more beautiful in person."

"Mr. B promised to take me someday. He's dead."

"That's hard, I know. I'm on my way to the bakery for some coffee and a pastry. I thought you might like to join me."

He smiled big. "Mr. B let me have two pastries. One to eat at the bakery. One to take home."

"Then that's exactly what we'll do."

"I'll get my umbrella."

"You won't need it. There's a beautiful blue sky outside."

"Rain is like life. It surprises you."

He raised himself up and tottered slowly to his apartment for an umbrella.

I pulled up to the bakery and parked in the spot where Bob had been skulking in his car.

I put a hand on Felix's arm. "I know it makes you sad to talk about the day Mr. Baumgarten died."

"It doesn't make me sad."

"Oh. Well, that's good then."

"It doesn't make me sad because I don't talk about it."

"Okay, I'll make a deal with you. When we leave the car and go inside, I won't talk about the day Mr. B died. I promise."

Felix was staring out the window at the bakery. "Mr. B let me sit at the table by the window. We watched people walking on the street."

"Then that's where you and I will sit."

"I like you." He smiled shyly.

"I like you too. We'll have coffee and pastries, and before we leave you can pick out a big bag of treats for your friends."

"For everybody?"

"Yes."

"I have a gazillion friends."

"It's a good thing they have a gazillion treats."

Felix laughed.

"Here's the deal. Before we go inside, tell me one thing about the white van. We'll make it a game."

"I like games."

"Me, too."

"I don't like this game."

I put an arm around his shoulders. "Please try just once. Close your eyes and remember the van. When you're ready, tell me one thing you saw."

He closed his eyes for what felt like a long time. When he opened them again, they were big with wonder.

"The bird! I forgot about the bird."

"Where was the bird?"

"In the van, silly. A blue bird. With sparkles." He laughed. "I like sparkles."

"Me, too."

"And a red tail. I did good, huh?"

"When you closed your eyes, did you see the driver?"

Felix smiled, proud of himself. "I saw the bird."

I forced a smile. My great idea a bust.

He twisted around in his seat and grabbed his umbrella from the floor behind him.

"Game over! Let's go inside."

I glanced in my rearview mirror as a sage-colored BMW pulled in behind me. The driver's face was familiar. He stepped out of his car and sprinted across the street. When he entered Baumgarten Jewelry I blinked twice.

I knew that guy.

I pointed at the glove compartment. "Gimme my spy-eyes."

Felix dragged the binoculars from the glove box and slapped them in my hand. I focused my gaze on the ex-cop with the man cave and ashes on his mantle. He investigated the Baumgarten jewelry heist. And now he was talking to Rob.

"Cam Stewart," I muttered.

"Are you a secret spy?" Felix said.

"I am."

"Cool. Can I see?"

I passed the binoculars and he held them to his eyes.

I realized I needed to take it down a notch. My initial surprise when Cam entered the jewelry store had been an overreaction. Yesterday's visit with the retired detective triggered a whirlwind of memories. It made perfect sense for him to stop at Baumgarten's. And he'd requested updates as the investigation progressed.

"It's nothing," I said. "I thought I knew that guy."

Felix stared through the binoculars.

"Cam the Ham," he sang.

I looked at him. "Why did you say that?"

"That's what Mr. B called him. Cam the Ham."

"Are you saying Danny knew Cam Stewart?"

"Mr. B knew everybody."

I tried the spy-eyes again. Rob Baumgarten and Cam Stewart faced each other. Their body language was intense. They appeared to be arguing.

I passed the binoculars. "Are you sure you saw him with Danny?"

He put them to his eyes and giggled. "That's the Ham, all right. Mr. B said he trusted to throw him far."

I thought about that. "Did he say he could trust Cam as far as he could throw him?"

"That's what I said."

I took the binoculars again. The two men seemed to have resolved their conflict. Cam extended a hand and Rob took it. Cam put an arm around his shoulder and hugged him. If he and Rob were friends, why lie? Cam made a point of making us believe they weren't.

Daniel Baumgarten had a son, Cam had said. What's his name? Ron or Rick?

Rob, Rocco told him.

That's it. Rob, Cameron said.

The guy was full of shit.

"Ready for some pastries?" I said.

Felix grabbed his umbrella and jumped out on the curb. I snatched my own from the trunk.

"You're right about rain being like life," I said. "I'm surprised all the time."

◇◇◇

Felix was good company and his eyes got all glassy when he ate his Danish. I washed mine down with two cups of black coffee. When I caught Cam leaving Baumgarten's I excused myself for a minute and met him at his car.

"Hi, Cam," I said.

"Cat!" His eyes darted across the street. "What are you doing here?"

"Having lunch with our good friend, Felix." I waved to Felix in the window. "Don't you want to say hi? He knew your name."

"I never met the retard, but I can tell he's a freak. If he's flapping his jaws, he doesn't know what he's talking about."

I wanted to slug him.

I jerked my head at Baumgarten Jewelry. "Visiting an old friend?"

"A victim of an unsolved crime," he corrected me. "I stopped by to talk about the robbery."

"What was his name again?" I blinked my eyes innocently. "Ron? Rick?"

"Robert."

"Ah."

Cam leaned in and his steel eyes bore through me. "I checked up on you, Ms. DeLuca. You're not a cop. In fact, you're nobody. You chase cheaters. Pathetic."

"I'm proud of the Pants On Fire Detective Agency," I blurted and my cheeks burned. I realized how lame that sounded.

Cam the Ham shot a demeaning smile and opened his car door. "You'd be well advised to stay out of things that don't concern you."

◇◇◇

I was crazy about Felix by the time I dropped him at home with treats for his gazillion friends. He blew me a big kiss from the door. It made me laugh. And it made me want to sock Cam in the kisser.

"I remember one thing about the white van," he called to me.

"Cool."

Felix laughed. "It was blue."

He disappeared inside. I stared at the door a while before snatching up my phone. I called my brother.

"Yo," Rocco answered.

"Do me a favor?"

"You got it, Sis."

"Get me Cam Stewart's service records with the Chicago P.D. Application, citizen complaints, any disciplinary action. And whatever bio you can get."

"Whoa. Take a step back. Cam is one of the good guys. He's not the enemy."

"What happened to 'you got it'?"

"I lied. Cops don't go after cops. Cam Stewart is off limits. I'm not gonna sully a cop's reputation."

"That's crazy talk."

"What the hell are you stirring up here, Cat?"

"A messy can of worms. I'm looking for a connection between Cam Stewart and Rob Baumgarten. Maybe they were teammates. I know Rob played soccer in college. And Cam has a few trophies on his mantle."

"I played soccer. Every guy I know played soccer. This is about the ex-wife, isn't it? You don't like Cam because he threw her furniture on the curb."

"I don't like him because he's a douche. And there's the thing about the wife's ashes in the tin cup."

"Cam said that cup is most valuable thing he owns. His wife is the douche."

"Wow, Bro. Your courage is staggering when Maria's not around."

Rocco laughed. "You got that right. What's really happening here?"

"Cameron Stewart knew the Baumgartens before he investigated the robbery. I think Danny didn't like him. He called him Cam the Ham."

"Okay, so they knew each other. I don't see a problem."

"And I wouldn't either if Cam hadn't gone out of his way to lie about it."

"That could be a problem."

"Your good buddy is hiding something. Don't you want to know what it is?"

"No." He blew air. "Dammit, Cat."

"Something's not right. I feel it in my gut."

"I hate your gut."

"I love you too."

Click.

◇◇◇

I tossed the phone on the seat and it vibrated before I kicked the car in drive. It was Chance. I killed the engine.

"Hey," I said, "are you on your way?"

"Sorry, Babe. Something's come up. I don't know when I'll get out of here."

"What's happening?"

"We got a tip. We think a fugitive is living on a boat at the marina. A sixty-four-foot Princess yacht; it's a real beauty. The boat's name is, get this, the *Mr. I Free*."

"I guess he won't be free for long."

"This is our second attempt to bring him in. My partner and I had him six years ago. He faked a medical emergency and we took him to the ER."

I swallowed a smile. "He slipped through the fingers of Special FBI Agent In Charge Chance Savino? How did that happen?"

"You're cracking up. It's not funny."

"Okay, Babe. I'm ready. I've got a stone face."

"My partner and I watched the techs put him in the MRI machine. They were instructed to call us when they were finished and we'd remove him from the tray. I waited outside the door. My partner ran down to the hospital cafeteria for coffee and sandwiches. When it seemed to take too long, we busted in. Our suspect was gone and two techs were unconscious on the floor. One was in his underwear."

"What about the guy who walked out the MRI door while you ate ham and cheese?"

"It was turkey and provolone. I thought the tech was responding to a CODE BLUE announcement. He had a radio to his face and hustled like he was off to save somebody's life."

"His own." I was in stitches now.

"You're enjoying the most humiliating moment of my career way too much."

"It's not you. Your fugitive is hilarious."

"He's a barrel of laughs."

I was having a good time. I couldn't help myself. "You said the name of his boat is *Mr. I Free*. Mr. I as in MRI. Your fugitive is MRI free."

He winced. "I missed that, too. God, I hate this guy."

"Payback, Babe. Go get 'em and laugh all the way to the county jail."

"We'll go in after dark. This could take a while. I love you."

"Remind me when you get home. Wake me."

I heard him smile. "Did I tell you how amazing this plonker's boat is? I just might have to take it for a spin."

◇◇◇

The gang of thieves would be desperate and running out of time. Their plan to snatch Captain Bob's dog had gone horribly wrong. The man I called Ponytail was dead. Their furry hostage was gone. And their last hope to save Saleen's dying mama had a forty-thousand-dollar price tag.

I figured they'd almost certainly do something stupid. If there's one universal truth about families, it's the utterly astonishing things we do to save the ones we love.

I swung by Connie's Restaurant on Archer and ordered a chop chop salad and an icy lemonade to go. Then I parked down the street from Pop's big, yellow house and kicked back the cushy seat. The loaner my mechanic calls Marion had generous leg room and a built in bum-warmer. It was a better surveillance gig than the dodgy Dreamscape Motel.

I eavesdropped on Pop's kitchen and ate my supper. The bug I planted could hear a pin drop. It came in a basket of super cool spy stuff from two super ex-spies. It was my best birthday present ever.

The kitchen was quiet when I tuned in. A muffled TV game show was playing in another room. I was slurping the last dredges of lemonade when hurried footsteps trotted on the hardwood floor. Water ran in the sink. And then the tinny clang of pans and maybe the chopping of veggies. A woman sang snitches of Pink. *Raise your glass if you are wrong in all the right ways...*I love that song.

Saleen was cooking dinner.

I rifled through my bag and pulled out last Sunday's *New York Times* crossword puzzle. I thought I was a freaking genius with puzzles until I met Rocco's wife. Maria and I have a weekly crossword competition and girls' night out. The loser buys a pitcher of margaritas. The wait-staff at Del Toro have learned to bring me the tab.

There were more footsteps on the floor and Pop's resonant voice. "Something smells good. What's for dinner?"

"Chicken Divan and rice. Mom's recipe."

"I hope she can eat tonight."

"Is she sleeping?"

"Not yet. I was reading to her."

"Is Aunt Becky coming?"

"After work. She'll be here around ten."

"When do we go in?"

My ears burned. *Where?*

"Eleven or so. I went over your pics. He has four cameras inside. Two on the street. And there's an ATM across the street."

"It's a smash and grab. We'll be in and out in sixty seconds."

"Not you. You're in the car. We agreed."

"I'm still driving. But we lost Marco. I'm going in with you. Besides, I gotta replace my necklace. That bitch ripped it off my neck."

A sense of dread squeezed my chest. They were going to hit Baumgarten Jewelry tonight. It was a stupid idea.

"Pops, if there's trouble we'll both get out. That bastard owes us. They killed Uncle Clive. No way he wasn't involved."

"I know, Saleen."

"You knew but you didn't go after them."

He gave a low chuckle. "Your mother laid it out for me. I couldn't have it both ways. It was her or the guys who whacked Clive and pinched our rocks."

"You chose her."

"And you. There ain't that many diamonds in the world."

"But you're breaking your promise now. What will you tell Mom?"

He blew a sigh. "If we're lucky she'll never know."

"And if she does?"

"We pray to God the treatment works. She'll have a long time to get over it."

I tossed the crossword puzzle on the passenger seat and killed the audio. My mind was spinning. Could the third man in the bogus 1999 robbery be Clive, the mother's brother? Saleen said he had been murdered and their diamonds stolen.

Was he talking about the diamonds the armored car delivered the morning of the delivery? Our assumption had been that the robbery was a staged, an insurance fraud. Were the bandits paid in diamonds and had Rob planned to steal them back? Was the brother's death part of Rob's original plan or an unintended accident? It was clear the family blamed Clive's death on Rob Baumgarten. But then maybe these guys were delusional. They were blackmailing Captain Bob and Papa for stealing a gold medallion they'd never seen.

I drove to Palmisamo Park and slipped my feet into running shoes. In the heart of Bridgeport, Palmisamo is a story of urban sustainability. Once a quarry and a landfill for clean construction waste, it's been transformed to nature trails, terracing wetlands, a fishing pond, and twenty-seven acres of sweet escape from the city.

I ran along the crushed stone path and mulled the events of the last few days over in my mind. I ran the hills until the stench of death left my nostrils and the air smelled like spring prairie flowers. When I knew what I had to do, I drove home and poured myself a glass of red wine.

Then I called the smartest man I know.

Chapter Twenty-three

The GPS locator I'd slapped under Saleen's car began moving on the screen of my iPad at eleven-twenty.

"Showtime," I said. "They're coming."

"I'm ready for them," Roger said.

He popped the last bite of *sfogliatella* in his mouth. His large frame swallowed much of the front seat. The only thing bigger than Roger's belly is his heart.

I gave him a quick hug. "Thanks for doing this." I could see him blush in the glow of his laptop.

Roger's screen was split in sixths, each frame with a live feed of Baumgarten Jewelry. My computer geek hero hacked into the two street cameras and we set up the other four. A camera faced each street entrance to the alley and there was a view of the back and the front door.

A MINI Cooper turned into the alley and the headlights dimmed. The driver killed the engine at Baumgarten's steel door and two masked bandits hit the ground running. One clutched loot bags in purple latex hands. The other brandished a flat-head ax and Halligan. Pops swung the ax over his head and Roger tapped a key on his computer. A deafening scream pierced the night. The security alarm exploded. Shop lights flashed. A police siren wailed and the would-be thieves bolted. The little Cooper peeled away before its doors were closed.

A chuckle spawned deep in Roger's throat and spiraled. He

threw his head back and had a good belly laugh. He's contagious. I laughed until my stomach hurt.

"Enough," I said. "You're killing me."

I poured two coffees and we finished the last two donuts in companionable silence.

"You can't always save people from themselves," Roger said.

I hooked his arm in mine. "But we did tonight."

He smiled. Do you think they're coming back?

"No way. Go home. I'll hang around a few minutes to be sure."

Roger settled his bum into his seat and the car rocked under his weight. "I'm not leaving until you do." He yawned.

Roger's ability to nap anywhere is legendary.

"What about Ginny?"

"She's in bed with an arm around Thor. She won't know I'm gone."

"Yes. It makes perfect sense that she would confuse you with a ten-pound Pomeranian."

"It's my hairy back."

Roger rubbed his eyes and yawned again. I yawned too.

"Stop," I said.

Roger grinned. "This is my first stakeout. I'm glad you called me."

"You're good company."

"Why me? You could've called a tough guy like Max. Or Savino. I'm more of a…"

"Adorable teddy bear? I suppose. But to be honest, I'd rather spend a long, tedious stakeout with a guy who makes me laugh."

"Thanks, Cat."

"Besides. I knew you'd bring donuts."

I didn't remember closing my eyes, but I was roused by fingers tapping my window. I jolted to consciousness and a sharp pain stabbed my neck. I was crushed against the door with Roger's incredibly, heavy head asleep on my shoulder.

A genius has a lot of gray matter.

Tap. Tap. Tap.

The car windows were a blur of fog. I swiped a circle of condensation away with my sleeve and peered through the circle. Narrow tight hips, hard abs, tight, muscular thighs. I'd know that, delicious hunka man-flesh anywhere.

I wriggled a bit. "Roger, wake up."

"Huh?"

I pushed him off me and opened my door. Savino popped his head in and growled. "If I didn't know you got it bad for Ginny, I'd think you were moving in on my woman."

"Cat?" Roger laughed nervously. "That's ridiculous."

"What's that supposed to mean?" I demanded.

Roger stammered and Savino laughed. "It's two a.m. on a South Chicago Street. Apart from the drool on her shoulder, I'd say you're keeping her safe. Thanks, man."

"Any time."

"But I'm going to have to fix you up with a gun."

Roger paled. "Guns kill people."

"That's the point," Chance said.

Roger gathered his computer and scrambled onto the sidewalk.

"Thanks, Roger," I said. "You did good tonight."

Roger's face flushed with pleasure. He piled into his Mercedes and we watched him drive away.

Savino took my hands, lifted me from the car, and kissed me. A tingling sensation warmed my lips and traveled south.

"Hmmm. Did you get your Mr. I Free?"

"Locked away and screaming for medical assistance."

"Did he say how he escaped the MRI machine?"

"He said he's a goddamn Houdini."

"Not tonight." I smiled. "How did you know I was here?"

"Your car wasn't in the driveway so I tracked your phone."

"Seriously?"

He laughed. "I'm starved. I brought Chinese. Kung pao chicken, dim sum, and egg foo yong. Whatya say I take you home, run a hot bath with lots of bubbles, and massage your sore neck?"

I managed a smile but my mouth felt flat on my face. "It could be a while before I'm ready for a bath."

He finger-smacked his head. "Marcus Russell. I'm sorry, Babe. That was stupid of me."

I wrapped my arms around him and pulled him to me. "How 'bout we go home, I get you out of that shirt, and take you to bed?"

"And just like that, I'm not hungry anymore."

A car engine fired up somewhere behind us. A moment later, a sage-colored BMW hammered by. The windows were dark and I couldn't make out the driver. But a chill shot down my spine.

Savino's head turned sharply. "Who was that? Was that car following you?"

"I don't know. I could be mistaken. For a minute I thought it was the cop who investigated the jewelry theft."

He gave me a light kiss. I could taste the relief on his lips. "Cops are the good guys, Babe."

"So Rocco keeps telling me."

"And they don't drive BMWs."

I didn't remind him Uncle Joey drives a Ferrari.

"If we're done here," Chance said. "I'll follow you home."

I climbed in behind the steering wheel. "Hey, how was the *Mr. I Free?*" I said. "Did you take her for a spin around the lake?"

The smiling cobalt blues crinkled around the edges. "Babe. You know that's against the rules."

Chapter Twenty-four

I missed Inga and I wanted her to come home. That's a good thing. Her time with her grandparents is best kept short and sweet. Inga is a food whore. And Mama is an orgy enabler. Papa hand-feeds my beagle from his plate. After two days with the grandparents, Inga waddles to the car.

I arrived at my parents' house as Mama hurried Inga out the door. Her trunk and backseat were packed tight with Italian cream cakes and *sfogliatella* for the school for tonight's auction.

Mama's face lit up when she saw me. Inga ran circles around my legs and Mama touched my cheek.

"Caterina! My angel."

"Uh, oh."

"Chance's mama called last night."

"I can show you how to block her calls."

Mama laughed. She has exciting news. "The Savinos are having a, uh, event next week. Family is flying in from all over the country."

My face twitched. "What event?"

"A cruise on the lake. Dancing. Fireworks. Catered dinner. The whole shebang. The family wants to meet the love of Chance's life."

"I'm going to be sick."

"I think someone has an anniversary coming up," she said slyly. "What could be more romantic than a moonlit cruise with the people who love you most?"

"An F-4 tornado cruising Bridgeport?"

Mama giggled. "Father Timothy will be on board."

Instant F-4 migraine. I massaged my temples.

"Kill me now," I said.

"Father Timothy is prepared to give Chance a priestly nudge about *you know what.*"

"Don't say it."

"Making you an honest, Christian woman."

I covered my ears. "You said it."

"That young man of yours should know you won't wait around forever. He's not the only starfish in the sea. My divorced dentist wants to meet you."

"Please. Tell me he's not coming."

She laughed and I groaned.

Mama reached into the backseat and pulled out a cream cake. She thrust it in my arms.

"Take this to Peggy and Captain Bob. Maybe she'll forgive you for making her come home when her sister needs her."

"But Mama…"

She made that clicking sound with her mouth. "And go to confession. The poor woman's lady parts were falling out."

Mama crossed herself. I felt my teeth grind.

She kissed her grand-dog and before I could count to ten, she was gone.

I drove to Captain Bob's house and carried the cream cake to the door. As my finger was poised to ring the doorbell, I caught a glimpse of Peggy Maxfield through window. I moved in and pressed my face to the pane. She sat on the flowered couch and she held Sam I Am on her lap. Her head was buried in his soft hair and her small shoulders shook with sobs.

I left Mama's cream cake on the porch.

◇◇◇

I hurried back to Jack's Toyota Corolla and hopped inside. Inga stood in the passenger seat and her breath smelled like bacon. Her tail wagged wildly and her eyes darted from the backseat to my face and back again. My partner was trying to tell me something.

This couldn't be good.

"Okay," I said, "whoever you are. Come out of the backseat before I shoot."

"Bitch."

I twisted my neck to check the floor behind me. A green scarf and mass of honey wheat hair.

"Seriously, Saleen?"

She caught her breath.

"How do you know my name?"

I turned to Inga. "Bite her!"

She joyfully wagged her tail.

"You're fired," I said. "When someone breaks into the car, you're supposed to bark. If she offers you bacon, attack."

Saleen crawled onto the backseat and jabbed something in the small of my back. "Keep your hands where I can see them or I'll shoot. I've got a gun."

"Ha! No you don't."

She dropped her hand.

"But I do!" I smiled.

"A 9mm Glock. It's in your panty drawer at home."

I gasped. It's just as well she was in the backseat. I couldn't reach her neck.

"You broke into my house?"

"Yes. Yes, I did." Saleen laughed.

I stammered." B-but I have a premium platinum alarm system."

"Then you were screwed. If it makes you feel better, your house was a bit of a challenge."

"A little. You must have mad skills."

"Thank you."

"You might as well sit up front with me."

"Just drive. We're not friends.

"I figured that out when you tied me up."

"After you ganked my necklace."

"After you snagged it from Rob. I returned it to him."

She gave a hard laugh. "As if he's not the biggest ferret of all."

"What's that supposed to mean?"

"What? Do I have to spell it out for you? Just drive."

I studied her face in the rearview mirror. Her eyes were swollen and she'd missed a mascara tear.

"Buckle up." I started the engine and took Canal Street toward Chinatown. I usually enjoy the drive, but today was garbage day. The tireless procession of bins and black plastic bags was a bit off-putting.

"I'm sorry about what happened to Marcus."

Her lips parted in surprise.

"I saw you at the Dreamscape. Is that what you wanted to talk about?"

She shrugged. "I saw you there. Tell me what happened."

"The police are in the early stages of the investigation. But they're treating it as a homicide. We'll know more after the autopsy."

"I talked to a maid. She said she found him." She shuddered. "Poor Marco."

"Do you know if he had enemies? Someone who would want to hurt him?"

"No way. He was a really good person, ya know? Everyone liked him." Her brow furrowed. "I suppose it could've been… Red light!"

My right foot pounded the floor. "No brakes!"

"Stop!"

"Hang on!"

I sped through the red light, horns blaring, and whizzed past the sickening crush of metal.

Saleen slapped my shoulder. "Stop the car!"

I was powerless. We seemed to be flying and the traffic ahead was stopped at the light.

She slapped my head. "Red light!"

"Hang on!"

I steered onto the sidewalk and piled through the long line of garbage. I grabbed Inga and held her tight.

Bam! Crash! Pow! It sounded like a cheesy Batman episode.

The impact of bins slowed or cut our velocity but two hefty dumpsters finished the job. My airbag exploded. I punched it out of my face and checked Inga. She smelled like bacon and she was fine.

"Saleen, are you okay?"

"Are we dead yet?"

"We're fine."

She took a deep breath. If she was counting to ten, she only made it to three.

"You're a maniac!" She slapped my shoulder.

"Stop hitting me."

"I will *never* ride with you again."

"Who asked you?"

I shoved my door open and stepped tentatively onto the pavement. Something whacked me from behind.

"Ow!" whirled around.

A very old and fierce Asian grandmother waved her flowery purse at me. "Look what you do! Garbage everywhere! Who clean this mess?"

I looked behind me and cringed. Chinatown could've been ravaged by a tornado. It wasn't noon yet. I had a feeling this was going to be a very bad day.

"I'm sorry. I couldn't stop the car. My insurance will arrange for a clean-up."

Her purse twitched. "Do not hit me again," I said.

She took a step back. She may have seen the crazy in my eyes. "I call police."

"Thank you," I said.

"You go to jail."

"Fabulous."

She stomped away muttering something that sounded as if she put a curse on me.

"Too late!" I said.

"I'm alive!" The rear door opened and Saleen climbed cautiously out of the car. "You! You are a maniac."

"The next person who hits me, gets tased. I am just sayin'."

"You're a freaking whack-job. I'm outta here." She tromped off, a little unsteadily at first, dodging garbage and talking trash.

"Saleen, wait! You should get checked out at the hospital. I'll pay for your cab home."

"You've done enough!"

"You were going to tell me who killed Marcus."

A woman watching from her porch hurried her children inside.

Saleen didn't look back. She answered me with a finger.

I walked around Jack's car and assessed the damage. The car's front end was scrunched like an accordion.

"Oh, Marion," I said. "Crap. Crap. Crap."

I braced myself and called my mechanic. He picked up on the first ring.

"Jack's Auto Repair.

"Hi, Jack. It's Cat."

"Caterina! I ordered the window for your Accord. You can have it back this afternoon."

"Fabulous."

"How's Marion?"

"Not as good as we'd hope. Here's the thing to remember."

"What thing?"

"Actually two things. First, I'm okay. No one was hurt. And Marion is with Dorothy now."

Jack choked. If there were words behind his choking gasps, they were indiscernible.

"The second most important thing to remember is that it wasn't my fault."

Jack yelped like a madman. I jerked the phone away and rubbed my ear. He has a thundering loud potty-mouth.

"I'm sorry. I'm not saying it's your fault. But there may have been something wrong with Marion's brakes."

A new torrent of creative curses came across the line.

"Okay, Jack. Those are very bad words. I'm not even sure what some of them mean."

Click.

"Jack?"

Suddenly the adrenaline crashed and I was a mess. My knees were rubber. I tried to punch Rocco's number on my cell and my fingers felt like wet noodles. I sat in Marion and held Inga. We listened to the wail of approaching sirens. The cops closed in. As the first flash of blue appeared, my phone bleeped. It was Max.

"Can I buy you lunch?" he said.

I opened my mouth and one shaky word came out. "Help."

Chapter Twenty-five

These cops were from the Twelfth Precinct. They didn't know me. They liked me almost as much as the Asian woman with her flowery bag.

I hugged my partner. "Toto, we aren't in Bridgeport anymore," I said.

The cops took one look at the long splatter of stinky garbage and demanded a sobriety test. I refused. Mostly because I didn't trust my legs to walk a straight line. But also because they were jerks.

The stocky cop with the square jaw took my license, registration, and Jack's insurance information.

"Caterina DeLuca," he said. "Is this your address in Bridgeport?"

"Yes."

"Are you related to…?"

"Yes."

"And…?"

"Yes. All of them."

He didn't mention a sobriety test after that. Maybe he still thought I was stinking drunk. It didn't matter. Cops protect each other's own.

Max tore up in his new Jag and pushed through the yellow police tape. The patrols didn't challenge. Special Forces training and sheer size gave Max an aura of authority. He pulled me up to my feet and held me against his chest.

"Kitten, are you alright?"

"I'm fine, really. Inga too. We were lucky."

"You made a helluva mess." He petted my partner. "What happened?"

"I lost my brakes."

"How bad?"

"Totally. They're gone. Zilch. Nada. Zip."

Max plucked the keys from his pocket and switched on a small flashlight attached to his keychain. Then he dropped to the ground and bent under the car. His hard muscular thighs and booty flexed, as he bent to adjust the angle of his flashlight. That man could fill a pair of jeans. Right then I knew I would be fine.

"Caught ya looking," he said.

My face warmed. "Was not."

He laughed softly.

It took less than five minutes. I heard him swear under his breath.

"Alright, Kitten, who'd you piss off this time?" he said.

"Nobody."

"Right."

He reappeared and scrambled to his feet. His jaw was tight.

"It's been cut."

"Cut?"

"The brake line."

"That's creepy."

"It's a message. Someone wants you dead."

"That's a helluva message."

"Can I take you to the hospital?"

"I just want to go home."

"Let me check your pupils for a concussion."

I opened my eyes wide.

"Hmmm. Your eyes are very green."

"Stop."

"Oh, my God."

"Is it a concussion?"

"No. But I can tell you were looking."

I pushed him away and he laughed. "The tow truck will drop Marion off at the garage. I'll talk to Jack. You might want to stay away from him for a while."

"I'd like to apologize."

"Send flowers. First we'll swing by my place and you can take my Hummer."

"I was thinking more like the Jag."

"You're adorkable."

"It's a faster getaway."

"The Hummer is safer, Kitten. You piss people off. You want to be in a tank when they start shooting."

◇◇◇

I didn't intend to follow Cam Stewart when he passed me heading north on Morgan Street. I was driving home in Max's Hummer, sporting Ray-Bans, and feeling almost bulletproof. I had a bag of Swedish Fish and two pints of Ben & Jerry's in the back—both of the decadent chocolate family. It had been a rough few days. I wanted to be home and I wanted my fluffy comforter to swallow me up and I wanted to take Inga and my two favorite guys to bed with me.

And yet, there I was, three cars behind Cam's BMW. I was chasing after him like a crazed stalker. The fact is I had no good reason to follow the ex-cop, apart from the fact that I don't like him. I don't trust him. And I suspect he twists the heads off kittens.

And with every skulking mile, Ben & Jerry were melting in the back.

Maybe Captain Bob was right. I need therapy.

Cam exited on Thirty-Second Avenue and picked up a six-pack at a corner Ma and Pa's, He locked the beer in his car and jogged across the street to a trendy café and sat at the counter. I parked in the grocer's parking lot and switched the cool shades for spy-eyes.

Cam drank coffee and ate a Danish. His glance strayed to a wall clock and the door. He was waiting for someone. My spy-eyes were smooshed to my face and I didn't see the late-model red sedan park across the street. But I felt the driver's squinty eyes and I dropped the binoculars in my lap.

Awkward.

He was beefy and bald and well dressed. He opened his door and Gucci stepped onto the street. He strolled into the diner and took the stool beside Cam. He whispered something in Cam's ear and when he cocked his head my way, I melted into my seat like my ice cream.

Their exchange was brief. The beefsteak dropped a fat envelope on the counter and exited the diner. I hid my face in yesterday's paper until I heard him drive away.

Cam opened the envelope and thumbed the contents before slipping it in an inside jacket pocket. He reached for the bill, and my partner and I bailed.

"One quick stop before we go home," I told her.

I dropped by the church and lit a candle for Ponytail.

While I was there, I said a prayer for Saleen's mama. It was a wish for forty g's to come her way.

◇◇◇

By the time I got home, my neck felt sore from my big kiss with the airbag and my muscles were stiffening. I drained the melted B&J down the sink, and recycled the containers. I brewed a soothing pot of herbal tea and gave Inga a sausage. After I banished the hair dryer from the bathroom, I drew a hot, lavender bath.

The jets made lots of bubbles and the swirling water eased the tension in my back and neck. I tried not to think about Ponytail's pruny toes and fingers. I thought about the white van and the blue bird and wondered if my friend Felix was a little nuts. I thought about the man in the black hat and the fat envelope he slipped Cam. And mostly I wondered what happened to the gold lion with emerald eyes and a mane of canary diamonds.

Rob said the medallion had belonged to Daniel's grandfather whom he was named after. It had been a gift for the grandfather's bar mitzvah and then for Danny's. I guessed the medallion referenced the story of Daniel in the lion's den.

I scooted out of the tub before my toes were pruny. I nuked the leftover Chinese and shared it with Inga by the fire. When I figured Saleen had found her way home from Chinatown, I drove to The Flower Cottage on Thirty-first Street and bought a bright blue and yellow bouquet. Then I parked in front of the big yellow house and tromped to the door with my flowers.

The doorbell played a chime. There were heavy steps and a man with thick gray hair and matching gray eyes smiled at me. It had to be Pops.

"May I help you?"

I shoved the flowers in Pop's hand. "Hi. My name is Cat DeLuca and…"

Saleen shot behind him. "It's her! Close the door! She tried to kill me."

I ducked under Pop's arm and pushed my way inside. I placed the flowers on a table and planted my bum on a soft comfy couch.

The gray eyes smoked. "If you tried to hurt my daughter, you'd best leave. Now."

"I did no such thing. Someone cut my brake line. I avoided a collision and kept her safe."

"Is that true?"

Saleen grumbled under her breath.

"I apologize for my daughter. This is a stressful time for us."

"I shouldn't have barged in like this. I was hoping for a moment of your time."

"Don't say anything," Saleen said. "She's got a wire."

I popped up and raised my arms. Pops wandered into the kitchen and Saleen gave me a ridiculously thorough search. I giggled when she poked under my arms.

"Enough already," I said. "I come in peace."

"She's clean," she called, and Pop returned with three glasses of iced tea. The ice cubes made a musical clink when he walked.

Saleen's green eyes flashed. "Tea? Are you serious? This woman forced her way in. We could shoot her."

"We don't have a gun."

The tea was delicious. "Is the mint from your garden?"

"Yours is hemlock," Saleen said.

A frail voice called from the top of the stairs. "Saleen, is something wrong?"

"One of those religious freaks, Mother. She has to tell us we're going to hell."

"I didn't raise my daughter to be rude. Soften your tone and offer her a cool drink. It's warm outside."

I figured I'd probably never meet Pop's wife. But she was just about the nicest woman in Bridgeport.

"I'll help her back to bed," Pop said. "We can talk in the kitchen where we won't disturb her."

Pop climbed the steps to his wife. Saleen and I carried our drinks to the kitchen table and Saleen put the flowers in a vase. When Pops rejoined us, he looked weary.

"Why are you here, Cat?"

"I want to express my sympathy for the loss of your friend. I only met Marcus once. He was nice."

"Thank you. He was a good friend."

I paused a beat. "I know you and he were two of the three men who staged the bogus Baumgarten Jewelry heist."

"Get out," Pops said.

"You realize the statute of limitations was up a long time ago. If you play nice and help us get the guy who killed Marcus, the captain won't charge you with dog-napping or blackmail."

A hollow, bitter laugh burst from Pop's throat. "He wouldn't dare."

"You're wrong about Bob. He didn't take the medallion. Someone else got it. You can help me figure out who."

"You mean like a witness or a medic. I suppose it could've been somebody else. But it wasn't, was it?"

"What do you mean?"

"Your captain didn't argue when I demanded money. If he didn't take it, he would have said so."

I couldn't tell Pops the captain didn't know they were talking about jewelry. Bob was guilty of an unconfessed transgression and it wasn't stealing gold off a dying man. I had the dreaded feeling it was much worse.

"Is Sam okay?" Pops said.

"He's fine. You took good care of him."

"I love that little guy. If Bob ever needs…"

"That's probably not going to happen."

"I suppose not." He stared into his tea.

"Saleen said you never got caught. Just lucky?"

"I suppose my luck would've worn out. But I'll be honest with you. I haven't done a job in ages. Bad knees. I'm too old to climb through windows and outrun the cops. I got me a job driving a school bus during the week. I do a little security work nights."

"That's putting the fox in the chicken house. Tell me what happened the day Danny died."

"Don't say anything," Saleen said.

He threw her a look and she passed it on to me.

"We went back to collect what was owed us. Clive was hot. We get there and the no-good son wasn't around. Just the old man. We said the robbery was a con. His no-good son owed us our cut. You could see the old man wasn't in on it. He was pissed. He couldda spit tacks. And hurt, ya know? That his son betrayed him that way."

"I can imagine."

"And then it's like the old man figures it out. He knows where the son hid the stash. He walks over to this old grandfather clock, opens the glass door and there's some kinda false bottom in there. He sticks a hand inside and comes out with this gold neck piece. It's a lion and a bunch of jewels. You never seen so much bling."

"Is that all he found?"

"I figure it was all there in the clock. The diamonds that was delivered that morning, all the pieces we was supposed to have nicked. It's like the old man didn't care about anything else. But he was over the moon nuts about the gold lion piece. I guess he thought it was gone for good."

"It was a gift from his grandfather."

"The old man says, 'Tell me what my son owes you. I'll pay it.' Just like that. He wanted to make things right, then and there. And then Clive says, 'Forget the money, we'll take that gold medallion instead and call it even.' Clive could be a jerk like that. I can see how he would look scary to a guy like Mr. Baumgarten. I would've talked Clive down. I wouldn't have let him take it. But the old guy panicked. He takes the medallion and runs. We chase after him but…"

Pops closed his eyes and shuddered. "There was a lot of blood. I had nightmares for weeks."

"Was Clive your brother-in-law?"

"How do you get this stuff?" he said incredulously.

"I'm a hotshot P.I."

I was showing off a little.

"That's a sleazy profession," Saleen said as if hers wasn't.

"How did Clive die?" I asked.

"The cops said he OD'd, but that was bullshit. Clive didn't do drugs. He didn't have a track mark on him."

"I'd like to look into it. What's Clive's last name?"

"James."

"Is there anything you can tell me about the accident? The guy driving the van?"

"For a hotshot detective, you don't know so much. Here's what I'll tell you. Your captain and his good-for-nothing partner…"

"That's her dad," Saleen blurted.

His eyes narrowed. "So your coward pops sent you here to spy on us."

"Trust me. If Papa knew about you, he'd be here himself. And you wouldn't be looking so good. Here's where we are. Two partners were murdered. I'm investigating Danny's death and my brakes are cut. Your life could be in danger too."

"No."

"How can you be sure?"

"Because I didn't meet Clive's contact."

"But Marco did?"

"Once. I had a family. I didn't want to know."

"Smart decision."

"Clive's contact hooked us up with a dozen or more jobs. Our last job was the night he died. It was our biggest score ever. We were given an address and the combination to a safe. The safe had stacks of cash and jewels and some gold coins. Our take was three bundles of C's and a sweet bag of rocks. The diamonds alone would set us up for a few years. Marco and I took our cash home and Clive held onto the diamonds. He knew a guy who could move them. We never saw him again. When the cops found his body, the diamonds were gone."

"Saleen, when I asked you who could've killed Marcus, who did you think of?"

"Baumgarten. He's gotta be Clive's contact. I can feel it in my bones."

Pop rubbed the bridge of his nose. "After Clive died, Marco was scared. He didn't think his contact killed Clive but he would've known who did." Pop dashed an eye with the back of his hand. "They didn't have to kill Marco. He wouldn't rat anyone out. That's how he was. But in the end, he knew too damn much."

Chapter Twenty-six

I called my brother from the car.

"I need a favor, Bro."

"Sorry, Sis. I'm all out."

Rocco was a little pissy because I asked him to check out his new BFF, Cam Stewart.

"I need the name of the cop who investigated an OD, September '99. I have a few questions."

"What's the druggie's name?"

"Clive James. Here's the thing. I'm pretty sure he wasn't a druggie. Somebody got away with murder."

"Won't be the first time. Clive James. Got it. Who is he?"

"One of the three guys in the bogus Baumgarten heist."

"So two of the three are dead."

There was the crash of pool balls in the background.

Crap.

"Who are you talking to?"

My stomach churned. I knew that voice.

"It's Cat," Rocco said. "She says hi."

"Liar," I said.

"You're with Cam."

"And Jackson. We're shooting pool and drinking a few beers. I'd invite you but there's a reason they call it a man cave." Rocco roared as if he'd said something hilarious. He'd had more than a few beers.

"Forget it," I said. "I'll ask Bob."

"The captain?" Rocco roared again. "Good luck with that. I'll call you with a name later."

"Yeah. Thanks."

I hung up and an icy chill pierced through me. I couldn't shake the eerie sensation that Cam's dark eyes looked through me. It was time to steal my Glock away from all my Victoria Secrets.

◇◇◇

I found Papa in the backyard firing up the barbecue to burn more chicken.

"Hi, Papa. How are you doing?"

"A little better now that Sammy's home. I've hardly slept since this bullshit started."

"It's going to be all right."

"Bob said the man who kidnapped Sammy was murdered at the Dreamscape."

"I heard that."

"I didn't do it."

"Do what?"

"I didn't kill the asshole. I wanted you to know."

"Good to know. What happened between you and Bob is your own business. Rocco and I will make sure it stays that way."

"Bob's a good man, Caterina. He was my partner."

"I know."

"I'd do anything for him."

"Something tells me you already have."

He slapped some chicken breasts on the grill and smeared them with barbeque sauce. "Staying for supper?"

"Sorry. I have plans. Do you remember a detective named Cameron Stewart?"

Papa looked thoughtful. "I know who he is, that's all. He wasn't one to hang out or grab a beer at Mickey's."

"Were there any complaints filed against him?"

"Lots of cops get complaints. Cam could've had more than most. He wasn't one to play by the rules."

"I heard he hurt his back. Draws a disability pension."

Papa shrugged. "Maybe he hurt his back. Maybe he didn't."

"Tell me. My lips are sealed."

"Bob said Cam was under investigation by IA. When he wracked up his back and took the disability, they dropped their inquiry."

"So he dodged a bullet."

"There were serious conduct and procedural issues that would've opened his previous cases for scrutiny. It was a Chicago PD and public relations nightmare."

"He may have put away innocent people."

"It's not right, I know. But it's how the system works."

I kissed his cheek. "Thanks, Papa. Enjoy your supper."

"Mama will be home in a few minutes. She's buying a dress for that boat cruise." He shook his head. "Those women are cooking something up. Maybe you can get it out of her. I can't."

I kissed his cheek. "I know exactly what they're up to. That's why I'm leaving."

◇◇◇

Inga and I walked in the park and shared a sleeve of crackers and cheese. We had an early night planned that involved a good book, a new squeaky toy, and my two favorite guys. That's when I remembered I had dashed Ben & Jerry down the sink. As if nothing is sacred.

I lay on the grass and thought about the missing lion medallion with emerald eyes. It was clenched in Danny's hands when he bolted from the store. The first witness to reach Danny told Max she couldn't recall a medallion. Max believed her.

It seemed likely the medallion had been ripped from Danny's hand when the van struck him. Someone could have pocketed it. And yet it was curious, after all these years, that such an extraordinary piece hadn't found its way to auction.

The sun warmed my face and my eyes were heavy. I listened to children play and the intervention of parents preventing bloodshed. As I drifted off, a warm, smothering tongue lurched me back. Four happy feet pranced on my chest. I opened my eyes and caught Sam I Am in my arms.

Ellie Maxfield flopped beside me on the grass. She hugged Inga.

Ellie is Captain Bob and Peggy's daughter and one of my besties growing up. She went through a rough patch after high school and did a short stint in drug rehab. She turned her life around. Now she's a junior partner in a prestigious law firm downtown.

"How's work?" I said.

"Love it. I've never been so happy."

"You deserve it."

We watched a group of teenagers walk by. "I'm sending my parents on an apology cruise this year. I was a horrible teen, Cat. I hate that I put them through so much shit."

"You weren't horrible. You were simply growing up. It's a precarious process at best."

She smiled. "You're a good friend. You never judged me."

"I love you, girl. You're amazing. Bob and Peggy are enormously proud of you. Never forget that."

We clambered to our feet and walked around the park. Elle was silent a long time.

"Okay, so spill it. Something is stressing you out. I have known you all my life, and you have never been good at hiding your feelings." I smiled.

She gave a little sigh. "I dropped by today and Dad is wound tighter than I've ever seen. Mom's been crying. Something's wrong with my parents and I don't know what it is. They won't talk about it."

She got that right. I'd been hounding Bob and Papa for days and their lips were sealed.

Her lip quivered a little. "I think they could be getting a divorce."

It was so ludicrous I had to choke down a laugh. "Captain Bob and Peggy? Not a chance, girlfriend. Your parents love each other. They're solid."

"People change, Cat. You should've seen them this morning."

"They're dealing with a problem, obviously. But it's definitely not their marriage. You can trust me on this."

"I hope you're right."

"I deal with divorce and betrayal every day. It's what I do. I know when a couple's energy is disconnected and damaged. Your parents are planning a future. Bob talks about their retirement plans all the time."

Her face scrunched with worry. "What could it be then?"

I shrugged. "They might need a little time to sort things out. If they're gloomy in a week or two, call me. We'll do an intervention."

She smiled. "That's some serious role reversal."

I laughed. "Karma's a bitch."

"What should I wear to your moonlight cruise?"

I winced. "Have you no compassion?"

Elle laughed. "My mother figured it's another one of your mama's ambushes. You and Chance and a priest in the middle of Lake Michigan, and no way to shore."

"Trust me. I can swim."

"You have an amazing life. You have a successful career. And a serious hunka man-flesh you can boot home when you want. Why's your mama so obsessed with you getting married?"

"Revenge. Payback for thirty-four hours of excruciating labor. And then I poured ketchup and syrup all over her album collection when I was four. Maybe deep in her heart, Mama doesn't want me to be happy."

"You're funny. Or maybe she wants you two to be as happy and she and your papa are. I see how they look at each other."

"Right, huh? After decades, they still can't keep their hands off each other."

Ellie made a gross face. "Eeeuw!"

"I know," I smiled. "It's awesome."

Chapter Twenty-seven

We were almost home when my cell vibrated in my jeans pocket. It was Rocco.

"Yo!" He said. "I got a name and I didn't have to turn on my computer."

"So you're psychic now?"

"Let's say I have connections. You won't believe this. The detective who investigated Clive James' death was Cam."

"Imagine that."

"That's a stroke of luck, eh? He overheard us on the phone and he remembered Clive's name."

"I bet he did."

"I think Cam likes you."

"Really? I think he has a place for me on his mantle."

Rocco laughed. "Cam said stop by later or call if you have questions."

"Is he home now?"

"He's got a golf game. Tee time was six."

I checked my watch. It was almost six-thirty.

"Jackson says he'll go with you. He's got a man-crush on Cam's pool table."

I laughed. "Ya think?"

"Anything else on your mind?"

"Nah. I'll catch you tomorrow."

"You weren't gonna tell me about Marion?"

I winced. "It's a long story. I trashed Chinatown. I'll buy you lunch tomorrow."

"Bring a lot of money. I spent an hour trying to calm Jack. He's cut you off."

"God, no!"

"He says you insulted his brake work. He sent your window back to the dealership. And he won't fix your car. Ever."

I needed a paper bag. I was hyperventilating. "Maybe if I stop by and apologize again…"

"It's not safe. You'd have better odds driving Marion with no brakes."

"I can bring him a big Tupperware of cannoli. You know how Jack is with Mama's cannoli. It can drop him to his knees."

"Okay. This could work. Remember, set the cannoli by the door and run."

"Gotcha."

I stuffed the phone in my pocket and raced to my bedroom. I tucked the 9mm in an ankle holster and strapped it under my jeans. I stuffed my lock picks in my pocket and raced across Bridgeport to Cam's condo.

I parked the Hummer on the street and walked to the door. I rummaged in my bag. When an older woman opened the door from the inside, a key was ready in my hand. I held the door for her and took the steps, two at a time, to the third floor. I knocked on Cam's door and waited thirty seconds before letting myself in.

My eyes swept the room, taking in the pool table, glimmering trophies, and an autographed baseball from Babe Ruth. Cam did very well for a guy on a disability pension.

I rifled through his desk looking for bank statements or bills but was unsuccessful. Cam left no paper trail. His laptop was either with him or hidden away in a concealed safe. There wasn't time to find it. I found a ledger in a secret compartment under his bed with columns of figures and words that were in some sort of code. I photographed a dozen pages and tucked the ledger back where I found it.

I took in an obsessive number of selfies and electronics and sports mania with the growing conviction that Cam Stewart is a narcissist. His walk-in closet could well clothe a half dozen men. The sheer quantity of designer shoes was obsessive if not fetish. He appeared to have no interests outside of self-indulgence. There wasn't a thought-provoking book on his shelf. The ex-cop appeared to be, quite simply, the shallowest person I've ever met.

And then something tugged at my awareness. It wasn't a voice. It was more of a knowing. Cam the Ham was home. The sage-colored BMW was, at that moment, pulling into the garage. I'm not psychic and I don't have super powers. But I didn't doubt what I knew. To cover my bases, I said a quick prayer to San Malverde. The good saint helps thieves escape.

The late reddish-yellow rays of the day's sun streamed through the window and onto the mantle. It wasn't the gold trophies or the art deco throughout the room that hooked me. It was the light that danced on the battered tin cup that was somehow stunning. Almost calling me to it. Cam had said it contained his ex-wife's ashes. More accurately, it contained the burned remnants of their marriage certificate, her photos, and her art paintings. And yet it was the most valuable thing he owned.

I hit the stairwell as the elevator door opened. I held the door a crack and watched Cam lug his golf bag inside. My heart pounded in my chest. I gave a high-five to my angels and shimmied to the Hummer.

My world was magical that night.

I stopped by Uncle Joey's on my way home. He's the most magical person I know.

◇◇◇

I slipped into a Minnie Mouse tee and brushed Inga's teeth and then mine. I had a good book to read and a cup of hot chocolate by my bed. I tossed Inga a new chew toy from the basket in the hall closet. She leapt on the bed and I was half a step behind when the doorbell rang.

It was too late for Girl Scouts to sell cookies, and friends are considerate enough to call first. It had to be my outrageous, interfering, Italian family.

"Open up!" The voice belonged to my switched-at-birth sister. "Caterina, I know you're in there!"

I tromped to the window and peered through the curtain. No devil children. My Chihuly was safe.

"I can see you!" Sophie sang. She waved two pints of Ben & Jerry's.

I swung the door open and she swept inside with my two favorite guys. I could've kissed her.

That was a first.

"I'll get two bowls," I said. "Whipping cream? Nuts? A cherry on top?"

She giggled. "Why not? Billy Blanks can't see me now."

I handed her a blue glass bowl and she gingerly scooped a few teaspoons.

"Oh, Barbie," I said and she laughed.

"Where are the kids?"

"Peter took them to a movie and ice cream. I'm training tonight for my new job."

"Congrats, Sis! What's the job?"

She looked hurt. "I'm a detective, silly. With you. Remember?"

I shoved my dish aside, and sprayed whipping cream straight into the carton.

"I'm sorry, Soph. It's been a challenging day. I can't train you tonight."

"Not you. Max! We're going to the shooting range."

"It's a little late for that. Don't you think?"

"It's not like a date. But I think he is totally into me. What do you think?"

"Max likes everybody. Except terrorists. And I'm pretty sure ax murderers are up there too."

"Be serious. You know what I mean."

"Are we in seventh grade here?"

"C'mon, Cat."

"Okay. He doesn't like you in the way I think you mean."

Her mouth made a pretty pout. "Why not?"

"Because you're married," I reminded her. "You have children. And just about the most terrific husband and father in the world."

"I know. But Peter isn't like Max."

"And you can thank your lucky stars. Max is commitment-phobic. Peter would walk through fire for you."

"Max is *GQ* hot."

"Hotter than walking through fire? C'mon, Sophie. You're crazy in love with Peter. You two need some time alone together. Somewhere tropical where you can drink piña coladas and be naked."

She smiled. "So how do you know Max isn't in to me?"

"Stop."

I could feel my hands around her neck. We were in seventh grade. I had her on the ground and I was choking the stupid out of her in the school hallway.

◇◇◇

The moment Sophie left I called Max.

"Kitten. How are you feeling after your misadventure with Marion?"

"My neck was a little sore but I worked it out. Thanks for being there for me."

"Always."

"And for smoothing things with Jack."

"You might want to stay away from him a while longer."

"How long?"

"A year should do it."

"You said you'd take care of things."

"It's a process. He wanted five."

"We're doing good then."

"Hey, Sophie and I are meeting at the firing range. I can swing by and pick you up."

"Maybe another time. She just left. We have a problem and I need you to fix it."

"Name it. What do you want me to do?"

"Tell Sophie you're gay."

"I'm not telling your sister I'm gay."

"There's nothing wrong with being gay, Max."

"There is if you want to date women."

"Okay. Say something else. Why do women break up with you?"

"I don't know. I never asked them."

"Peter would've asked them."

"Peter's a good guy. I like him."

"He's in touch with his feminine side."

"I could be in touch with your feminine side."

I shivered and my voice was a squeak. "Tell her you're a selfish prick and you don't like kids."

"I like dogs."

"You can say that. I don't want her to think you're a monster."

"Anything else?"

"Yes. No matter what, don't take your shirt off."

"Why, for chrissake?"

"Because it makes it hard for a woman to breathe."

"I felt it under your sweater when I pinned on the pass. Do you mind if I see it?"

Felix smiled broadly and dragged out the medallion resting on his chest. He held it reverently in his hands.

"May I?" I asked.

He hesitated only a moment before removing it from his neck and lovingly placing it in my hands. It was heavier than I'd imagined. My fingers caressed the lion's face and the canary diamond mane shimmered. The emerald eyes mesmerized me. I realized I wasn't breathing.

I could imagine the thieves chasing Danny for the medallion. And I was certain Felix could be in grave danger if his secret came out.

"The lion takes my breath away," I said.

Felix smiled softly. He understood perfectly. "You won't take him away, will you?"

It was his turn to hold his breath.

I placed the medallion back in Felix's hands. "The very last thing Mr. B. did was give you your most important job. Keep it safe."

◇◇◇

My phone made one sharp ding and I checked the screen. I had a text from Uncle Joey. He was with his financial advisor and best friend, Bernie Love.

Last night I gave Joey the pics I took from the little black book I found under Cam's bed. He said Bernie would have a few things to say about the pages.

Joey texted: Hey Cat, Bernie said re/ ledger. C's been a very bad boy.

No surprise there, I responded.

My source tells me IA was investigating C for drug trafficking and protection when he took disability retirement. B says ledger is consistent with suspected activity.

IA dropped their investigation when C retired?

Hey. CPD doesn't need the freaking grief.

Got that. Thanks, guys. Anything else?

Yes. Stay the hell away from that AH. He's got too much to lose.

◇◇◇

I punched my brother's number on my phone.

"Yo!" Rocco said.

"Do I have to put a pool table in my living room to get your attention?"

"It wouldn't hurt. What's up?"

"It's about your buddy, Cam. He's a crook, Bro. IA was investigating him for drug-trafficking when he bolted."

"He didn't bolt. He had a disabling injury. Give it a rest, Cat."

"Uh huh. Bernie went over Cam's little black book."

Rocco groaned. "Tell me you didn't break into Cam's house."

"How else would I know he has a little black book?"

"I'm going to hate myself for asking. What did Bernie say?"

"He said the figures in the book are consistent with an illegal drug operation. You know what they say. Cops have the best dope."

"Dammit. He was talking about getting Jackson and me into his club."

"Watch your back, Roc."

"There could be a perfectly good explanation for all this. It wouldn't be the first time IA went after a good cop."

"You got that right."

"Maybe I'll be up front. Just ask him."

"While you're at it, ask Cam where he was the morning Ponytail was killed."

Rocco blew air. "Is this another one of your hunches?"

I felt my cheeks burn. "I guess."

"Cat, I'm hanging up now. You're beginning to scare the hell out of me."

Chapter Twenty-nine

I drove to Captain Bob's house with a pan of manicotti. Mama was worried about Peggy, and her solution to any problem is to feed it.

There was no answer when I rang the bell. I walked around to the backyard and found Peggy on the porch swing. She may have been sleeping. The swing swayed gently, her eyes were closed and her lips slightly parted.

I sat beside her and watched a pair of cardinals splash in the birdbath. She didn't open her eyes at first but she knew it was me.

"You and Ellie spent hours on this swing when you were kids," she said. "Do you remember the summer I brought the long craft table up from the basement and we did our projects outside on the porch?"

"I loved that summer."

"I miss those days."

"I didn't realize you got rid of your trampoline. Ellie and I practically lived on it that year."

"It was bumming me out. I was saving the trampoline and swing set for my grandchildren but I'm beginning to lose hope. If Ellie ever gets with the program, I'll buy new ones."

"That works."

"Your mama has lots of grandkids."

"Yeah. Sophie's uterus is gonna fall out."

She stared at the spot where the trampoline used to be. "You and Ellie are running out of time."

I laughed. "We're good. And we have plenty of time. But apparently my biological clock is screaming in Mama's ear."

"Next Saturday night, all the guests aboard the *Spirit of Chicago* will hear it."

I groaned and Peggy laughed.

"Your mama's nudging you in the right direction."

"Marriage? Been there, done that."

"Not with Chance, you haven't. Johnnie Rizzo was a putz."

"You could've mentioned that before I married him."

She laughed. "Maybe I was blinded by his good looks. Of all of Ellie's friends, you've been my favorite. So, let me give you a word of advice."

"Uh oh."

"Release your barriers. Go with the flow and quit rowing upstream. Relax and enjoy the cruise. Guzzle some champagne and eat a big, fat piece of wedding cake. See where Fate takes you."

I choked. "Wedding cake?"

"Did I spoil the surprise? It's an engagement party, of course."

"Traitor! You're in cahoots with Mama."

"Of course I am. Did you taste her Italian crème cake? This will be fun. You and Chance on a romantic cruise. Soft music. Champagne."

"And a hundred dysfunctional family members. It's not a cruise. It's a train wreck. The peace-loving, ex-hippie, anti-gun, vegan Savinos versus the bone-sucking, beer-guzzling, locked and loaded DeLucas. It'll be a slaughter."

Peggy laughed. "And I wouldn't miss it for the world. Your mama has chutzpa."

"Jewish women have chutzpa, Peggy. In a Catholic Italian woman with no boundaries and a screaming biological clock, chutzpa is a form of insanity."

◇◇◇

I helped Peggy pick lemon basil, a little rosemary, and a handful of oregano from her garden for a salad to accompany the manicotti.

"The coffee's fresh," she said as I traipsed behind her inside. The kitchen smelled yummy, like sugar and spice. Gingerbread, I guessed. When I leaned against the oven, it was still warm.

"I saw Ellie and Sam at the park," I said. "She said she was worried about you and Bob. She thought you were stressed."

Peggy spun around and searched my face. "What did you tell her?"

I shrugged. "Nothing."

She breathed again.

"Ellie looks good," I said. "She looks happy."

"She is. Bob and I are proud of her. She graduated from Northwestern in the top ten percent of her class."

"She always was the smartest kid in school."

Peggy filled two sunshine yellow mugs with coffee and put out a plate of cookies. Ginger cookies rolled in sugar.

"Yay," I said. "I love your ginger cookies. They were my favorite when Ellie and I were kids."

"I remembered. There's a bag on the counter for you to take home."

The brown paper bag had a purple bow and my name in bold, black marker. *Caterina.*

Peggy sipped her coffee and met my eyes. "I was expecting you."

"I didn't even know I was coming until this morning."

"Bob said you were investigating Sammy's kidnapping. I knew you'd figure it out."

"Oh."

"You were a clever child, Cat. Your mama used to say if you were a boy, you'd be Perry Mason or Matlock one day."

She's got one foot firmly planted in the twentieth century.

"I remember the year we had a magician here for Ellie's birthday party. You ruined the show. You exposed his secrets and pointed out the smoke and mirrors. You hid the rabbit he was supposed to pull out of his hat."

"I was awful."

"You were the most amazing kid I knew. Except for Ellie, of course."

"Of course." I smiled.

Peggy warmed our coffees. "How long have you known?"

"That you were driving the van that killed Daniel Baumgarten?"

She was momentarily taken aback. I thought the unspoken secret was harsh to hear.

"Bob and Papa were in the café across the street when your van struck Danny. They must've seen you flee the scene. They lied their socks off to save you. They bungled the investigation. They falsified witness statements. Maybe even eliminated a few. They reported the van was white. Not blue."

Peggy dabbed a tear with her napkin and placed it on her lap. "I'm so sorry, Cat."

"It was a lot to process at first. Since we were kids, Papa and Bob were our heroes. They were unwavering in their ethics. I've worked through it. They had their reasons and they made the best choice they could. They would do it all again. I can respect both of them for that."

Peggy wrung her napkin between her fingers. "Thank you."

"Why?" I said.

"Why, what?"

"Why run away? It's not like you. Or why not come back later and turn yourself in?"

"I, I…" She looked cornered. She'd had years to process this. To find forgiveness and closure. And yet she appeared startled and totally unprepared to answer my question.

"Why don't you tell me what happened?"

"A girlfriend I went to college with was in town. We met for lunch, had a few drinks."

"You were drunk?"

"I was buzzed. I left Chili Thai. I was driving north…."

"North?"

Peggy twisted her napkin. "Mr. Baumgarten came out of nowhere. I couldn't stop. I didn't see him."

There was the sound of a key turning a lock and the front door opened. Captain Bob's voice boomed. "Peggy! You have some very serious Girl Scouts out here selling my favorite cookies."

"You're on a diet, Bob."

A lemon crème donut diet, I thought to myself.

"Better hurry, Peg, before I buy every box."

"Excuse me, Cat. Bob needs his Samoas. And I'd better get a Thin Mint."

"My fave. Thanks for talking with me. I'll let myself out the back."

"You're sure? Are we good?"

I grabbed my bag of ginger cookies and hugged her. "Always. Welcome home, Peg."

She smiled. "We'll see you Saturday on your elegant, moonlight cruise. It should be exciting."

"That's what they said about the *Titanic*."

◇◇◇

Rocco blew me off when I did my Cam the Ham rant and it irked me. He usually respects my judgment. Or at least he listens to me. But my brother had been seduced by the keeper of the man cave. And the keeper's a jerk.

What I needed was rock-hard evidence. A bug. And one last peek into Cam Stewart's condo.

I punched my brother's number on my phone.

"Yo, Cat!" Rocco said. "What's up?"

"Nothin'. Just touching base with my Bro."

"Have you been drinking?"

"Coffee. Tea."

"Vodka. Don't drive, Sis. Call if you need a ride."

"So…whatcha doin'?"

"I just got off the phone. I left my wallet at Cam's and I won't be able to get it later. Frank said he'd pick it up for me."

"I can swing by for it."

"Not a good idea. Cam says you were following him. You had binoculars. You're starting to creep him out."

"They're really thick glasses. Cam sounds a little paranoid-schizo, if you know what I'm sayin'. Why not pick up your wallet now?"

"Cam has an all-day golf tournament. If you gave him a chance, I think you'd like him."

Like that's gonna happen. I was already running to my car.

"Gotta go, Rocco. Hugs to Maria and the girls."

Traffic was light and I shot across town to the amazing man's condo. I parked in front of a fire hydrant and propped a "Police Business" pass in the window. My brother is still looking for it.

I knocked once and waited thirty seconds before letting myself in. This was an in and out. I counted twelve quick steps to the mantle. An abrupt spin. And….ten, eleven, twelve steps out.

"Step back inside and shut the door."

The dark voice cut like a knife and sent a shiver up my spine.

I stood in the open doorway and gauged the distance to the stairwell. I considered making a run for it. I'm fast.

"I've got a gun."

Maybe not that fast. I spun to see if he was lying. He wasn't.

"Whoa!" I shielded my eyes. "Put on some clothes. A towel, anything."

It was the bald, beefy guy from the café. He was wet and soapy and hairy all over. He didn't finish his shower.

I closed the door, careful not to latch it.

"You really should rinse off," I said. "Soap will dry your skin."

"Great. A freaking comedian."

The revolver gestured to a chair at the bar. I sat.

He moved across the room and dragged a long, khaki coat from the closet. He tugged it on, one arm at a time, the pistol steady and staring me down.

"Uh oh," I said. "Somebody's waking up. Can you put that thing away and tie your coat, please?"

Beefy-boy reached in his pocket with his free hand and pulled out a set of handcuffs.

"Seriously? What kind of guy carries handcuffs in his pocket?" A pause. "Oh. Kinks and cops."

I didn't like either possibility.

He hardly spoke and I couldn't shut up. Fear winds me up like Chatty Cathy. So does tequila.

The side of beef walked toward me and suddenly I couldn't breathe.

"Give me your hands," he said.

I held out my wrists and he slapped on the cuffs. They tightened each time I moved my hands.

He took a step back and lowered the revolver a moment while he tied his coat.

"Now you just look like a flasher," I said.

At least he wasn't a kink. He was probably a cop. Well trained and athletic. It would be hard to get away.

He crossed to the mantle and picked up a phone. He punched in some numbers and held it to his ear.

"Hey," he said, "you have company. Get your ass home before I kill her."

There was a pause. "No. That is your job."

I couldn't breathe. My heart pounded in my chest. I looked left, and then right, my frantic eyes searching for a weapon. If I was going to make a move, it would have to be now. Cam was on his way. I wouldn't have a prayer against two.

He paced back and forth, the phone to his ear. Their exchange became heated and he let the gun waver in his hand. The next time he walked past me I booted a hard karate kick to the back of his knee. He buckled. I kicked his hand and the gun dropped. Somehow the wine bottle was in my hands. I planted a foot on the floor and belted a very nice Chardonnay into beef boy's groin. He groaned with pain and fury. I sprinted for the door but huge hands grabbed my foot and we were both on the floor.

He raised himself to his knees and hunched over me. He looked terrifyingly fierce and large. His eyes were insane. He bitch-smacked my face. A fist slugged my abdomen and I exploded in pain. He got up, recovered his revolver and aimed it at my head. His hand shook with fury. He wanted to pull the trigger and he was trying not to. I stared hard into soulless eyes. I couldn't stop him. But I wouldn't make it easy on him, either.

He lowered the gun and sat on the stool and watched me like a lion smelling blood. I lay on the floor panting for air. I thought I should pray but I couldn't remember the saints' names. Or any of the prayers. I willed the gods to not let me breathe my last jagged breath in this dreaded, godforsaken man cave.

After a while he got up and walked toward me. His face was distorted. He was still mad about the wine bottle and the balls thing.

"Get over yourself," I said.

My head was throbbing. My stomach was in agony. What else can he do to me?

A tortured sound came out of his throat and his big hairy foot punted toward my head. There was a flash of color. And then everything went black.

I shouldn't have asked the question.

◇◇◇

When I came around again, the keeper of the man cave stood over me, a curious expression on his face. I gingerly touched the lump on my head. That was going to hurt.

"Your buddy has anger issues," I said.

"He's an asshole. He left me to clean up the mess."

"Why are you staring at me?"

"Deciding how to do this one. How to dispose of the body. My partner suggested a sharp saw, garbage bags, and lots of bleach."

"That's just creepy. You should be getting good at this by now. Clive. Russell. Were there others?"

"Just two. You'll make three. They were scum. Not you. You're"—he searched for the word—"annoying."

"Do you mind if I sit up?"

He shrugged. "Be my guest."

I gingerly rose to my feet and moved to the stool I really wished I hadn't left.

There was a sound at the door. A metallic clink and Rob Baumgarten walked in. A horrified gasp escaped his lips. I was a bloody, beaten mess.

"Cam! What the hell are you doing? Put that gun away."

"Never mind about that. Bring the duct tape from the tool-box in the closet. Tie her up good. She's not going to ruin us."

"She can't ruin us. We haven't…"

Rob stopped mid-sentence and his face went ashen. "My God. What have you done?"

"Nothing for you to worry about. Duct tape. Now."

"Your pal, Cam, is a cold-blooded killer," I said. "He killed two of the three guys he hired to fake your heist."

"Is that true?"

"She's lying."

Rob picked up Babe Ruth's baseball from the mantle and examined the signature. "What will you do to her?"

"That's not your business."

"I'm not going to let you hurt her."

"Finally," I said, "a voice of reason."

"The bitch is a pain in the ass."

"That's a little harsh," I said.

"It's true," Rob said. "But she's not gonna die. This ends here."

There was a loud, harsh knock and for a millisecond, Cam's eyes shot to the door. It was all we needed.

I lunged at Cam, knocking him off-balance and capturing his ankles with my handcuffed hands. Rob hurled the Babe Ruth baseball and whacked his wrist. Cam yelped as the revolver flew from his hand and cartwheeled under the pool table. Cam vaulted after it and a flying gold trophy conked him in the head. I jerked the 9mm from my ankle holster and aimed at Cameron Stewart's chest.

Cam cradled his head. "You weak, miserable fool. I should've taken you out long ago."

I held up my wrists. Rob found a small key on the counter and removed my handcuffs. I walked over to the mantle and pocketed the phone I'd planted in the tin cup. I had the hard evidence I came for.

"You saved my life," I said. "Tonight you made your papa proud."

"That's gotta be a first," Rob said bitterly. "Do you know what it's like having a saint for a father?"

"Not really. We DeLucas don't have the saint gene."

There was another *knock knock knock*.

"My dad worked too hard to spend much time with me. But he did everything with that worthless punk. Gawd, I hated him."

"Who?"

"Felix. Did you know my father left him a trust? The punk has fancy digs. Everything handed to him. I had to scrape to keep afloat during the recession. Felix didn't blink."

"Felix was an abandoned baby. He deals with mental and some physical challenges. And yet, he's fun to be around. Maybe your dad didn't hang out with you cuz you're a selfish jerk."

"Whatever."

"Do you know what happened to your father's gold medallion?"

The pain behind his eyes was raw. "I was young, and ambitious then. I was a fool."

"You're a damn idiot now," Cam said.

"My father wouldn't finance a second shop. If dad got the insurance check, I could turn over the diamonds and jewelry to start out on my own. I didn't intend to take the medallion. It was in the shop for a cleaning. I got greedy."

"Your father found where you hid the medallion."

Rob nodded miserably. "I don't know how or when. He left the diamonds and jewelry and only took his medallion. He must have hated me awful."

I didn't tell Rob that it was the stolen medallion that sent Danny running to his death. I figured Rob had enough guilt to reconcile. When you're a selfish prick, it's hard to find a path to peace.

"Why don't you get that duct tape?" I said.

He fetched the duct tape from the closet and we secured Cam to a chair. Then I gave Rob a quick hug.

"It was getting ugly in here before you came. Thank you, again, Rob. Now get outta here before the cops come."

Rob ran out the door and my crazy Cousin Frankie wandered in. He stared at me. And at the thoroughly duct-taped Cam.

And back to me again. There was a gun in his holster. I wished mine wasn't at my ankle.

Cousin Frankie rushed in. "Cat! What the hell are you doing? This man is a cop. He's one of us."

"He's a cold-blooded killer. Call it in, Frankie."

Frankie's eyes darted to Cam and back to me again as if deciding what to do.

"She's a liar," Cam said. "She's out of her freaking mind."

"She's been hit in the head a few times," Frankie said.

"And you have the brain of a freakin' flea," I said. "Call it in."

My cousin reluctantly dragged out his phone.

"Wait," Cam said, "I can pay you."

Frankie's eyes popped. He dropped the phone back into a pocket.

"Seriously?" I said. "You're going to go there?"

"There's diamonds, a fortune of diamonds in the tin cup on the mantle. Let me go and they're all yours."

"Don't listen to him," I said.

"You can have it all. Everything you always wanted," Cam said and his voice was as smooth as a snake. "You deserve it, Frankie."

"You got that right," Frankie said.

"It's a slippery slope," I said. "You don't want to end up like this guy."

"Filthy rich?" Frankie barked a hard laugh. "Like hell I don't."

He crossed the room to the mantle and took the battered tin cup in his hands. He stuck his fingers inside. Then he tipped the cup upside down.

"No diamonds," he said.

"B-b-but," Cam sputtered. Hatred spewed from his eyes and there was venom in his voice.

"You—you bitch! You're not going to get away with this."

I leaned close and whispered in his ear.

"I already have."

◇◇◇

My stomach ached where beefy-boy slugged me. I could feel

it bruising. I walked out on the balcony and hit my brother's number on the phone.

"Yo!" Rocco said. "What's up?"

I heaved a sigh. "It's about your buddy, Cam…"

It was a short conversation.

"Rocco and Jackson are on their way," I announced when I returned to the man cave.

"Frankie," Cam said in a snake voice, "there's a hidden safe in the bedroom closet. Let me go and take it all."

Frankie's tongue wet his lips.

"If you even think about it," I said, "I swear I'll shoot you."

Frankie gulped a nervous laugh. "You knew I was kidding about the diamonds back there, right?"

"You're a piece of crap, Frankie. What did you think would happen to me after you freed that douche bag and danced away with your diamonds? You couldn't think he'd let me go?"

"I didn't mean it. I swear. You're not gonna tell the family, are you?" He swallowed hard. "Or Savino? Or Max? Or Tino?"

Frankie slumped in a chair and buried his head in his hands. "I'm a freaking dead man."

I cut the edge from my voice. "Don't worry, Frankie. I won't tell them."

He raised his head and his eyes were drenched in self-pity. "Honest?"

"Honest."

His voice broke. "Caterina, why are you so damn good to me?"

"Because after I tell Cleo, no one will ever find your body."

Chapter Thirty

Captain Bob and Papa and Uncle Joey and I paused on the curb and blew a collective sigh. Then we trudged up the steps to the yellow house.

"We don't have to do this," Uncle Joey grumbled. "That asshat kidnapped Bob's dog, you know what I'm sayin'? I know somebody…"

"You are somebody," I said and hooked his arm. 'Play nice."

Pops opened the door and his face turned a pallid green. His eyes darted back and forth in primal flight mode.

"Cool it, Pops," I said. "We come in peace."

I pushed past him and took a seat on the couch. The others followed and made themselves comfortable.

Saleen sailed in from the kitchen with a pot of tea and three cups. She could've dropped the tray when she saw us.

"You might want to get more cups," I said.

Her throat went dry. I knew this because when she spoke her first words were a croak. "You don't want him. Take me."

"You're both more trouble than you're worth. If you took my dog, I'd…"

I jabbed Uncle Joey in the ribs.

"We don't want either one of you," Papa said. "We're here to talk. Off the record, so to speak."

"In other words," Captain Bob said, "we're not here."

"That must mean I'm not about to puke," Saleen said.

Papa's hand gripped the scar on his bum but his gaze was steady. He held Pop's eyes. "Bob and I did not take the lion necklace."

"Medallion," I said.

"Whatever," Papa said.

"If you say so." Pop shrugged. He believed him like he believes in Santa.

"I know a guy," Uncle Joey muttered.

Captain Bob cleared his throat. "The Chicago PD has taken a second look into the death of your brother-in-law, Clive James. The original cause of death has been amended. Mr. James was the victim of a homicide. A suspect has been arrested and will face charges."

Papa added, "We deeply regret that it's taken so long for the truth to come out. Please express our condolences to your wife. Her brother will finally have justice."

It was too much for Pop. All the bluster was sucked out of him and his legs crumpled under him. He flopped into a recliner and a tear coursed down his cheek.

"I still want to kick your ass for taking Sam I Am," Papa said, "but something good came from it. We wouldn't have known about Clive if you hadn't."

Pops blew his nose hard. "You're welcome."

"So, who killed my Uncle Clive?" Saleen demanded.

The captain sighed heavily. The people of Chicago would eat this one.

"The suspect we arrested is Cameron Stewart," he said.

Pops went bug-eyed. "The detective who investigated Clive's case?"

"It wasn't CPD's finest hour," Papa admitted.

"Why kill him?" Saleen demanded.

"For the diamonds," Pops said. "Looks like Cameron Stewart was to be Clive's contact. That son of a bitch! That's why Clive's charges were always dropped. He had a dirty cop in his pocket."

"Cam didn't want to kill him," I said. "He planned to fake a mugging and grab the rocks. But Clive recognized him and Cam panicked. He killed him."

Pops swore under his breath.

"My Caterina recovered the diamonds from Cam's apartment." Papa was bustin'-his-buttons proud. "She says there's a highly effective, but expensive treatment, that could help your wife. And your share, after the insurance, is forty g."

"Your ransom demand for Sam I Am," Captain Bob said. "I should kick your ass."

"This is on Cat," Uncle Joey growled. "Personally, I would've kept the rocks and got a sweet beach house in Soverato."

Uncle Joey tossed a fat certified check to Pops. "I called in a favor and liquidated the diamonds for you. You got an exceptional price."

I drew a pair of teardrop diamond earrings from my pocket and dropped them in Pops' hand. "I kept two fat rocks out for Rana. Rob set them for me. I figured it was the least he could do."

It was all too much for Pops. He couldn't speak. His fingers trembled and the check dropped to his lap. Saleen picked it up and gasped.

"How did you find the diamonds?" she said.

My grin was a stickler. "I went to church and lit a candle for Rana. I said a prayer for forty g's and the angels went nuts."

Uncle Joey snorted. "Go to church and light a candle for your Great-Grandpa DeLuca. He bootlegged whiskey with Al Capone. He could know where Scarface hid his gold."

"There'll be enough money left over for Saleen to go to school and quit being a screwup," I said. "And Pops, your bad-boy days are over. I have a pic of you raising a flat ax to Baumgarten's back door. Don't make me show Rana."

"How can we ever repay you?" Pops choked.

"We'll buy her freaking driving lessons," Saleen said.

Chapter Thirty-two

It was late when I strutted into Tino's Deli. The dinner rush had passed and a few stragglers lingered over a bottle of wine. A server with frizzy red hair wiped down tables and chairs for the night.

The ex-spy's face lit when he saw me. "Caterina!"

He hustled from behind the counter, took my face in his hands, and kissed my cheeks. "The investigation, it is finished?"

I nodded.

"Bravo. Sit. I have a nice Cabernet."

I took a table by the window and watched the slow procession of white and red lights through Bridgeport. Tino hung the *Closed* sign on the door and selected a bottle from the wine rack. He opened the bottle and filled our glasses.

The ex-spy clinked his glass with mine. "What is spoken here, stays between us."

"Gotcha."

"Who killed my friend, Danny?"

I sipped some wine. "It's complicated."

"I want it all. Why did he run into the street?"

I gulped more wine and pulled a leg up under me. "The three men from the armed robbery returned to the shop that day."

"To rob Danny again?"

"No. To collect their money."

"The gleam in Tino's eyes was freaking scary. "Are you suggesting the burglary was a scam. Insurance?"

I nodded.

"I'll kill that greedy bastard."

"Rob had company. Cam Stewart. You know him?"

"He's a dirty cop. Danny hated that Rob hung out with him."

"Birds of a feather. Rob hired these guys and then shorted his partners. Instead of shelling out their agreed share, Rob paid them in tacky, flawed diamonds and cheesy cubic zirconia. It was a fatal mistake."

Tino's teeth ground. It was a lot to take in.

He reached into a pocket and dragged out a flask. He tossed down a drink and passed it over.

I did the same, then handed it back.

"Danny was shaken to his core when the thieves told him Rob betrayed him. He offered to pay Rob's debt right then. One of the thieves got greedy and frightened Danny. He wanted his grandfather's medallion."

"The medallion was a family heirloom. No one messes with Danny's lion."

"Danny ran with the medallion. I think he was blinded by grief and rage. He never saw the van."

"Who are these scum who killed my friend?"

I dropped a hand in my lap and crossed my fingers. "Clive James died shortly after Danny."

"Lucky bastard."

"Clive's death was ruled an overdose. The truth is, Cam Stewart killed him for a fat swag of diamonds and cash. Cam was the first responder and he was assigned the case."

Tino hissed. Cam Stewart is a snake."

"Marcus Russell was killed at the Dreamscape Motel. Bathtub, hairdryer, 220 volts of electricity. It was awful."

"Cam again?"

"Bingo. When we began investigating the Baumgarten armed robbery, Cam knew we'd eventually identify the three guys on the security film. Marcus wasn't a rat. But he could connect Cam to multiple thefts and possibly to Clive's homicide. It was a chance Cam couldn't take."

I slugged down the rest of my wine. "Cam's in the clink. The prosecutor hasn't decided what to charge him with. It's a political time bomb for CPD. Maybe he'll hang himself in his cell."

"If they want him to die in a crash on a lonely stretch of road, I'm their guy."

"Do spies go to heaven?"

"Spies are God's angels. Who's the third guy?"

I dropped my second hand in my lap and double-crossed my fingers. I bugged my eyes wide open. I read once that people blink when they lie. And I was lying through my teeth.

"Tom Barker. He died a few years ago in Joliet. Cancer."

"Was it slow?"

"Excruciating."

"Good."

Tino passed the flask and I took a good pull of whiskey. It was a good burn.

"What will you do about Rob?"

"I'll deal with him later."

I almost felt bad for the guy. "Danny will be watching."

"Dammit."

"You should know that Rob saved my life tonight."

"Christ, Caterina. What happened?"

"Last night I let myself into Cam's condo…"

"Where was Max? You promised to take him with you."

"I was an idiot. Are you finished yelling yet?"

"For the moment. Continue."

"Anyway, Cam is laundering money for some wanna-be-gangsters. I needed more evidence. I surprised one of his buddies in the shower. Cam came home. They argued over who would kill me. Luckily for me, Rob stopped by. He knew nothing of the murders and the blackmail. When he couldn't stop Cam, he tackled him. He risked his life. And he was willing to face prison to save me. He showed a lot of chutzpah."

"Dammit. I can't kill anybody, can I?"

"I think Danny would want you to give Rob a chance to turn things around."

"Rob can make his papa proud. After I kick his ass."

"Did Max tell you Rob's a fence? He buys stolen jewelry."

"Not anymore. Rob is having a come-to-Jesus moment."

"Isn't he Jewish?"

"Right. So he's coming to Yahweh if I have to drag him there." Tino grunted. "Now, I want the driver."

I felt a knot in the pit of my stomach. "It wasn't the driver's fault."

"Danny was left to die in the street."

I stared at my wine.

"Forget about it," Tino said. "I don't need to know."

"Really?"

I felt almost giddy with relief. I popped out of my chair and hugged him tight.

"Tony and Bob can keep their secret," he said. "It won't bring Danny back."

I leaned back searched his face. The gold flecks in his brown eyes danced.

"You crafty old spy. How did you know?"

Tino winked. "I haven't forgotten the extraordinary things we do to save the ones we love."

We finished our wine in peaceable silence before he walked outside with me.

"One more thing," he said before I slid behind the wheel, "you didn't say what happened to Danny's gold medallion."

Crap. "Uh…"

The corners of Tino's mouth twitched. He was smiling inside. "Don't tell me if you have to cross your fingers again."

Epilogue

Blue is Chicago's color. There is no blue like the blue you'll find in this city. Not the white or the dirty gray you'll have to suffer through in order to endure our godawful winters. You won't stay long in this city if that's what you remember. But if you do stay, you'll fall in love with this city, and it will be because of Chicago's blue nights.

And this was one of those nights. The sky was darkening toward sapphire as Chance wove his way through Streeterville toward the lake. The city lights sprouted gold and pink halos. As we approached Navy Pier you could see the fluffy green trees and the white sandy beaches of Chicago's lakefront. Beyond lay the luminescent aqua blue of Lake Michigan stretching to meet the sapphire sky on the horizon.

Chance parked in the west garage, jumped out of the car and came around to let me out.

"Have I mentioned how devastatingly gorgeous you look tonight?" He held out his hand and I stepped out of the car. His eyes took a leisurely stroll from my taupe caged leather stilettos, up my legs to the asymmetric hem of my white dress with silver-white lace overlay by Marc Jacobs. It had a high neck. It was modest enough for meeting Chance's relatives but it hugged me in all the right places. The lack of cleavage didn't seem to bother him at all.

Chance lifted my hands to his lips and kissed the bruises on my wrists. The deep purple handcuff marks had softened to a hideous green and yellow. Tonight I'd covered them with wide silver bracelets. I heard enough snickers at the grocery store.

He gently pulled me to his chest and kissed me. His lips were soft and warm and a little groan escaped my throat.

The cobalt blue eyes crinkled. "Let's get away next week. I found a little beach house in Turks and Caicos with a four-night cancellation."

"Sounds divine. But I'm busy next week. I've got a date at the Lincoln Memorial with the new man in my life."

"Felix Proust," he said. "Should I be jealous?"

I shrugged. "He makes me laugh more than anyone. But then, you have other qualities."

"Like what?"

"There's that thing you do with your tongue."

"This?"

His lips traveled to the curve of my neck and I gave a little shiver. I wrapped my hands around his back and lay my head on his chest. Nothing else seemed to matter.

"Later," he whispered and breathed in the scent of my perfume.

"If we escape now, we'll be in Canada before the vultures know we're gone."

Chance gave a low chuckle. "Come on. Let's get this over with."

"Oh. So now you're the grown-up one."

He took my hand and we walked out of the garage into the glistening lights of Chicago's most popular attraction.

Navy Pier is a massive phallic symbol jutting out just short of a mile into Lake Michigan. During World War II it was used to train pilots to land on carrier ships. I'm told the lake floor around Navy Pier is littered with planes that didn't make the landing. George H.W. Bush received his carrier-landing training here.

Today, Navy Pier is a destination site with its massive Ferris wheel, sight-seeing tours, botanical gardens, shops, restaurants, and year-round exhibitions. Fireworks light up the summer and fall nights and a massive indoor skating rink can ease a long Chicago winter.

Navy Pier is also where you catch the flippin' boat that your boyfriend's damn parents have viciously scheduled for an intimate dinner cruise with fifty interfering guests and a drunken priest.

As we strolled onto the deck, tour boats and cruise boats lined the side of the pier.

We were looking for the *Spirit of Chicago* and it wasn't hard to find. The fourth boat in line had a crazy Italian woman in a cream dress and sensible shoes hanging over the guard rail, frantically waving a hankie. Mama.

"Catarina! Catarina! Woohoo!"

"Ignore the crazy woman."

"Catarina! I *see* you! Don't think I don't *see* you!"

Chance grinned and lifted his hand to wave an acknowledgement.

The party had already started. "The Otherside" by Red Sun Rising was blaring from the boat. Mama turned her back to us, trotting toward the gangway shouting orders.

"They're coming! Everybody! Listen up! I want that music *OFF*."

Mama's voice cut those decibels like butter.

Click.

As Chance and I took our first step up the gangway, Bruno Mars' "Marry You" magically oozed out of the sound system at a reverent volume. My eyes shot up to Mama who stood at the top with her folded hands clutched between her breasts. Chance's mom stood beside her. Both of them gazed down at us with that sappy starry-eyed look pasted on their faces.

Kill me now.

"Champagne for everyone!"

Stewards with trays hustled through the crowd offering champagne in fluted glasses. The Savinos, a refined, elegant bunch sipped, while most of the DeLucas were double-fisting the drinks.

I took a quick inventory of the crowd. Father Timothy knocked down a glass and grabbed another before you could say "water into wine." Next to him was Mama's geeky dentist. For an instant, our eyes met and I gave an involuntary shudder. He looked hopeful in a really icky way.

Chance hooked a couple of glasses and turned to me. His face was closed and serious as he handed me a glass and lightly took my elbow. He steered us through the crowd toward the bow where I saw Chance's father standing with a clutch of smartly dressed, attractive people. They looked a little shell-shocked standing there, holding a single glass apiece. These were obviously not DeLucas.

I felt a collective sigh of relief as Chance turned on the charm and started making introductions all around. Aunts, uncles, and cousins gazed at me with cobalt blue eyes, the edges crinkling in a familiar way with happiness and warmth.

We drank more champagne and the conversation became easy. No one mentioned the E word or why they'd flown all the way here for a lake cruise. They wanted to give us the supreme joy of making the announcement ourselves. They were here to celebrate "our moment." They were all so likeable, so accepting, so refined, so *classy*. Not one of the aunts eyed the width of my hips to gauge my childbearing potential.

Behind us the DeLuca bash was in full swing. The bass sent vibrations through the bottoms of our feet in time with the music. Champagne flowed like Niagara Falls. The twins each tilted a bottle to the sky in a speed race to see who could guzzle a bottle first. There was loud, drawn out belching followed by boy giggles.

Captain Bob's daughter tromped over in a black sequined maxi dress with a slit up the thigh. "Hey, gorgeous," I said.

Ellie hissed in my ear. "How dare you, Catarina DeLuca. You're the one who upset my parents. Leave my mother out of this!"

"Don't do this, Ellie. You and I have been friends forever."

Ellie dramatically spun on her heel and stomped away.

"I know you were driving that day," I said.

Ellie froze and I went to her.

"Geez, girl. We were what? Fifteen? What happened?"

"Billy Bonham and I played hooky from school. Some band was in town and Mom was away for the day. It was late. I dropped Billy at home and I heard this horrific sound. Steel crushing bone and flesh. I still hear it today. I have nightmares. If I saw the hit, I don't remember. Is it possible to block out something like that?"

"I dunno. Talk to someone who can help you, El."

"I was scared. I drove home and told my mom. She put the van in the garage and then one morning it was gone."

A server floated by and Ellie grabbed two glasses of bubbly and handed one to me.

"Thanks."

She tossed hers down. "How did you know?"

"It was the blue bird. Your mom had after-school craft projects for us. You remember the bird we made out of papier mâché? With a red tail."

"And a ton of glitter."

"A friend of Danny's witnessed the accident. He saw it hanging from your mirror. He didn't see you. He saw the bird."

She smiled. "Guess that's a dead giveaway."

"First I thought your mom was driving. A few things didn't add up. And then she said she was driving north."

"I was going south."

"Yeah."

Ellie hugged me tight. "You're the best friend I ever had." She held me a moment and I heard a little gasp.

"Come to Mama," she breathed.

"Huh?"

She grabbed my arm and spun me around. "Who's that hunk of gorgeous?"

She was ogling Max.

"That's Max. Ex-Special Forces. Ex government spy. Just about Tino's best friend. Drives a Hummer and a spankin' new Jag."

"Will my parents like him?"

"They'll love him."

"Dammit."

She fluffed her hair and licked her lips. "How do I look?"

"Gorgeous. Go ask that delicious man over there to dance with you."

Ellie crossed the room from the left as Sophie, my switched-at-birth sister, swept in from the right. Sophie saw Ellie going for Max and she started to run. But Ellie had long, determined legs and a long, dry spell without a man between them. She reached Max first, attached herself to his arm, and hung on.

I could read Ellie's lips. *Back. Off. Barbie.*

Sophie's shoulders slumped and her husband, Peter, swept in. He took Sophie in his arms.

"Good gawd," Papa said in my ear. "Are they doing the tango?"

"I believe they are."

"Who the hell is leading?"

"Believe it or not, Papa, it's Peter."

"It's disturbing to watch your daughter dance like that."

"Perhaps they could finish the dance in the Caribbean. If you and Mama will babysit, Savino can hook them up with a beach house."

"I'll ask her." He grabbed another champagne. "All these bubbles are giving me gas."

"Chance says there's good whiskey at the bar."

I took the glass from his hand and tossed its contents down my throat.

◇◇◇

There was the feedback of a sound system firing up and the captain's voice welcoming us aboard and announcing we would be casting off in ten minutes. We drifted back to the party and the Savinos started mingling around the edges.

Chance and I were immediately the center of attention.

"Have you set the date yet?"

"Your babies will be so Bee-U-Tee-full!"

"Gonna make an honest woman of her, eh?" Nudge, nudge, wink, wink.

I felt a little giddy and wondered how much champagne I'd had. I'd have to be vigilant lest I played into the devious mamas' hands.

Out of the corner of my eye I saw Mama shove Father Timothy through the crowd. Mama looked like the Wrath of God pushing his unwilling prophet into the belly of a whale. I looked up at Chance and caught him staring down at me again with that same inscrutable look I'd seen earlier.

The moral high road talk was about to commence.

Suddenly a piercing note sounded overhead. We all jumped and looked up. The boat's horn was announcing our departure. The crowd cheered, Champagne bottles popped. We felt a slight sway under our feet as the boat began casting off.

Savino pulled me to him and I lay my head on his chest. His heart beat strong on my cheek and my own fell in sync.

The sound system hummed back to life and a voice sounded overhead.

"Good evening, my name is Chad and I am your cruise director for this evening. On behalf of the crew and those serving you tonight, welcome aboard and thank you for choosing Omega Cruise Lines, the greatest cruise line on the Great Lake of Michigan!

"Tonight's route offers unparalleled views of our world-famous Chicago skyline. As we leave Chicago Harbor, we will begin north past North Avenue Beach and then swing about to the south. We'll be dropping anchor near the Planetarium and Shedd Aquarium, just outside Burnham Harbor, where you will enjoy the best view of our stunning skyline and this evenings fireworks from Navy Pier.

"Tonight's cruise is in honor of two people who are getting engaged tonight! Or is it a wedding? I've spotted a priest with us. And our custom three-tiered wedding cake has mysteriously been added as part of tonight's buffet!"

I slugged down my champagne and glanced up at Savino. The cobalt blues took my breath away.

The sound of a nearby horn cut into the night.

Savino smiled. "That's Stan. He's our ride."

I giggled. "We're escaping Mama's sabotage cruise?"

"Happy anniversary, Babe."

"Woo hoo!" I slapped a high five. "Who's Stan?"

"We were partners when our prisoner escaped from the MRI."

A thundering voice boomed over the boat's speaker. "Attention *Spirit of Chicago!* This is FBI Agent Stan Cross on the *Mr. I Free.* Cut your engines and prepare for two passengers to disembark."

I blinked. "You stole your fugitive's boat?"

"Temporarily. The feds always lose stuff."

Savino grabbed my hand and we pushed through the crowd to the port-side deck and leaned over the rail. A sixty-four-foot Princess yacht hugged our boat.

"Su-weet," I said.

Chance's ex-partner waved. He had a bad-boy smile and a fresh sunburn. He'd been playing pirate since he and Chance arrested their MRI fugitive.

Stan tossed up a rope and Savino secured it to the rail.

Papa dashed a tear from his eye. "Finally! They're eloping!"

I scrabbled over the rail and shimmied down the rope with Savino hot on my tail. Our feet hit the deck of the Mr. I Free and Stan jammed the yacht in gear. We were off and running.

Chance gathered me into his arms and kissed me. A long and slow kiss like savoring chocolate.

The *Spirit of Chicago* exploded with cheers. I decided the happy sobs were Cleo's. Maybe Frankie's too.

And yet, above all the hoopla, Mama's clicking sound cut across the water. Her shrill voice pierced the night.

"Caterina, come back! You forgot the priest!"

To receive a free catalog of Poisoned Pen Press titles, please provide your name, address, and e-mail address in one of the following ways:

Phone: 1-800-421-3976
Facsimile: 1-480-949-1707
Email: info@poisonedpenpress.com
Website: www.poisonedpenpress.com

Poisoned Pen Press
6962 E. First Ave. Ste 103
Scottsdale, AZ 85251

3/17